SIRENA

Vista, California
Journey Press

Journey Press
P.O. Box 1932
Vista, CA 92085

CREDITS
Interior art: Lorelei Esther, 2021
Cover design: Sabrina Watts at Enchanted Ink Studio

First Printing March 2021

ISBN: 978-1-951320-14-0

Published in the United States of America

JourneyPress.com

To Stefu, the original Sirena

SIRENA

Book 2 of the Kitra Saga

Gideon Marcus

Journey Press
journeypress.com

Chapter 1

The client still hadn't shown up. *She will show*, I told myself. She had to, or my whole career might be over before it had even started.

The *Majera* occupied just a tiny corner of the spaceport hangar. Around it were a dozen other vessels. Some of them were strictly in-atmosphere jobs, sleek hypersonic pleasure ships used by rich people to zip between Vatan's two continents. A few were big transports, dwarfing the rest of the ships like mother birds in a nest. The wedge-shaped form of *Majera* was innocuous and drab amongst the newer vessels. The other ship owners probably never gave it a second look.

To me it was beautiful. It was *my* ship. But would the client think so?

My footsteps rang hollowly as I walked up to the smooth hull and pressed my fingers against it. The surface was cool, automatically absorbing my heat and redistributing it evenly for quickest disposal.

"Nervous?" Pinky asked.

I looked over my shoulder. Pinky had three legs at the moment, as well as two arms and a stubby something one could call a head. At least, that's where he was keeping his eyespots, black swirly things that showed no emotion. But his rubbery skin was a deeper pink than usual, a sign of concern.

"She's still not here," I said, checking my *sayar* again. 17 minutes late. And no messages. The client hadn't included trace information, so there was no way to know where she was or even if she was still coming.

"Maybe she saw my picture and got frightened off," Pinky said, rippling his round body in a way he probably thought looked creepy. To me he just looked like a water balloon pulsing in slow motion, about the least threatening sight in the universe. Then again, I was biased. Pinky had been my friend almost as long as I could remember; he never looked scary no matter what shape he was in. Still, I had to keep in mind that most humans had never seen an alien before.

"The only thing about you that might scare someone is your sense of humor," I said with a forced little laugh.

"You just don't appreciate art," he said, punctuating it with a snort. Not a true snort. Pinky's whole body was his nose, for inhaling and exhaling.

Peter, sitting next to Fareedh on one of *Majera's* stubby wings with his big arms folded, called out, "Fake fart noises are art now?"

Pinky swelled slightly and waggled his hands like fans. "Who says they're fake?"

I felt my lips curve in a real smile then. But my feet returned to their pacing, making a small circular path in front of the ship. Would she come? Maybe it had just been some kind of joke. Why would a noble want to hire me, with just one hyperspace flight to my record and that one hardly a great success. Did it make sense hiring myself out for interstellar flights so soon? Maybe I should have limited my availability to in-system flights. After all, Yeni Izmir, Vatan's system, was an important one, and the most populated besides Sennet, capital system of the province. Plenty of destinations to take passengers or special cargo. And it'd be close to home in case any of the crew got cold feet and wanted off. After last time, I wouldn't blame them. On the other hand, we could make a lot more, a lot more quickly, with out-system Jumps. I hadn't named my ship *Majera*, Turkish for 'adventure,' because I wanted to stay home.

The chime from my *sayar* interrupted my thoughts. I was still gripping the thin device; I hadn't put it back in my pocket since we'd gotten to the hangar, I realized. A display rose above the device's flat surface, showing me the lobby of the hangar. There were two people: a middle-aged woman with dark hair, wearing a flowy purple outfit, and beside her, a small woman wrapped in a shawl, riding in a grav chair. I couldn't see her face, but she appeared frail. I had the impression of a frail old lady.

I looked over at Marta for reassurance. She gave me a warm smile and a nod, curls bobbing around her pretty face. Then I turned, ready to walk to the door to let the newcomers in, but the translucent portal against the back wall of the hangar had already irised open, and they were through. At first, they turned right instead of left, disappearing behind one of the bigger ships. I heard faint conversation in a language I didn't know, becoming louder as they emerged from the other side, this time facing us. I raised a hand shyly and waved.

"*Majera?*" the lady in the chair called out.

I cleared my throat. "That's us, Ma'am."

She glided soundlessly up to us, leaving her companion a pace or two behind. Then she reached for her shawl, bracelets tinkling at her thin wrists, and pulled it aside.

My breath caught at the sight of her, she was that lovely. Her skin was a deep bronze, maybe a shade lighter than mine. She also was not old. In fact, she might not have been more than a few years older than me. She had that not-made-up, made-up look I'd always been jealous of but couldn't be bothered to learn. Her ears went to delicate points. That might have been cosmetic, but it looked natural enough with her elfin features. Bright red hair tumbled over thin shoulders. It looked as if she wasn't wearing anything under the shawl, and I felt a flush come to my cheeks. Then I saw the sparkling of jewel-finish cloth, gauzy and brief.

I stammered, but she wasn't looking at me. She was looking over the ship with sharp, dark eyes. At last, she glanced over at me. "*You* are Captain Yilmaz?"

I shrank a few sizes in my jumpsuit, the most formal set of clothes I owned. For a crazy moment, I considered pointing to Marta and saying, 'No, it's her!' After all, Marta was nearly a head taller than me, considerably better dressed, and certainly more impressive. But I was the one wearing the silly hat, the peaked one with the visor Pinky had given me after the last voyage.

"Yes, Ma'am," I said.

"I see," she said. "Well then, I am Sirena Isabella de la Atlántida Jáimez. The Seventh."

The name didn't mean anything to me, but Pinky bowed deeply, his body creasing at the juncture of his legs and the rest of his him. Out of the corner of my eye, I saw Fareedh take to his feet and also give a courtly bow, his iridescent cape swirling. I followed suit jerkily.

"Your… Grace?" I asked, looking up at the woman in the chair.

She arched a noble eyebrow at me. "'Your Highness.' I am a princess of the royal house…"

I bowed more deeply. I hadn't been in the presence of nobility since I was a child. Now a member of the royal family was in my hangar.

"…of Atlántida, not the Empire," she continued. "Please, this display is unnecessary."

"Yes, Ma'am… Your Highness… Ma'am."

Her expression was unreadable, cold. "I shall get right down to business, as they say." She spoke good French, the Empire's official language and one of the two I'd grown up with, though she had an odd accent. The vowels were clipped. "I want to hire a captain to take me beyond the Frontier."

I blinked. Twice.

"Is this a problem?" she asked.

"No, Ma'am, it's just…"

"Just?"

I don't know what I'd expected when I'd put out the ad. The most romantic notion I'd had was that maybe we'd be contracted to take a special package all the way to a Cis-Frontier planet like Talvi, something a client wouldn't trust to the posts. More likely, someone would want a chartered flight to the provincial capital. But *beyond* the Frontier?

Peter had gotten up from his perch and joined us, a frown on his angular face. "Ma'am, Punainen's a week away as it is, and then there's getting across the Rift."

"I am aware of the topography," she said crisply. "This is a mission of importance."

A mission that would take weeks, no, months. I definitely hadn't planned on that.

"What is the mission, exactly?" Marta asked.

The princess pursed her lips as if trying to determine if it was worth the time to explain it to us or better to cut losses and find another crew. She nodded curtly and said, "Bueno. You see, Ms. Yilmaz, we are looking for a new world to colonize. Atlántida is, as you may guess from the name, almost entirely ocean. That's fine as far as farming and floating cities are concerned, but it's terrible for mining." Her fine-boned face took on a pained expression. "Ours has always been a poor world. Sadly, our ancestors did not have great luxury of choice when they settled there, as it was during the First Expansion. As for finding a better home, we have through trial and error learned that all of the good worlds with breathable atmospheres on this side of the Rift have been claimed. At least those within the Imperial reach, and we're," she smiled abruptly, "meaning the royal family, not just me," the smile disappeared, "we're not interested in waiting for the Grilchie wars to open up more territory. No, the place to go is beyond the Frontier, now that the Rift is crossable. I want you to help me explore completely new worlds, to help me stake a claim on a lovely new home for the people of Atlántida." Her eyes locked onto mine. "And we need to do it quickly lest we lose out on a good planet again."

My mind reeled. Colony wildcatting! Find the right world, and you were a trillionaire. *If* your ship could stand weeks away from home. *If* you didn't run into any trouble planetside. Dangerous work, but also exactly what we'd gone through on our first trip. Not that we had planned on it that time. I licked my lips. This was a lot more than I'd expected.

Pinky stepped forward and bowed again. "Your Highness," he said in as rich a baritone as any holo actor, "We would need to charter the Trans-Rift ferry. The Rift is 17 light years wide, and *Majera's* range is ten."

I glanced at my friend, then back to the princess. If she was at all taken aback by Pinky's strangeness, she didn't let on. She waved her hand dismissively. "Of course. I didn't think this tiny thing had a Type 5 on board."

I felt hot under the sleeves of my jumpsuit. *Majera* wasn't a 'tiny thing'.

Sirena continued, "Of course we shall pay the ferry fee and also for provisioning and—" she looked over *Majera* doubtfully, "whatever upgrades will be necessary to make the trip comfortable." She turned to me. Her eyes flickered to the top of my head, then to shoulders, to toes, and back up to stare at me directly. "You are very young, though."

Once again I felt small. In over my head. We were all young, none of us more than 20 years standard.

"That's true," I said with a downward look, feeling the opportunity slip away.

"But not inexperienced," Fareedh drawled from right beside me.

"Oh?" Sirena asked.

"It's a new frontier, Your Highness. Wide open and dangerous. You want a crew that's been to the unknown and back, overcoming odds by the skin of their teeth." A smile broadened on his lean, dark face, and his brown eyes danced. "That's us."

Sirena looked at him without emotion. "Go on."

"Just last mission we did an exploration run," he said. "We Jumped a full ten light years into untraveled space, to Jaiyk to investigate the abandoned base there. It's an empty system with no facilities, just like the ones we'll be scouting past the Frontier. We had to scoop our own fuel, take hostile planet precautions. It's all very familiar to us."

I suppressed a bewildered laugh. Count on Fareedh to spin a complete misfire of a flight, the *only* one we'd ever done, into a selling point.

It seemed to impress Sirena, though. With a slightly thawed tone, she asked, "And just what do you do on the ship?"

"I program the ship's *sayar*, Your Highness."

"And you?" she said to Marta.

"Life Support and Biology," Marta answered.

The princess eyed Marta a moment appraisingly. Then, "I like your earrings. Tuessa?"

"Oh no," Marta replied, her voice lighter. "Vuitton. I want to get a pair of Tuessas though. Are yours?"

"No, darling. These are from home."

Marta stepped forward for a closer look. "They're beautiful. I love the opalescence."

"There's a local nautiloid we harvest for the shell. Rare ones display this quality."

"Do you export them? Could I... could I get a pair?" Marta asked.

Sirena shook her head, and the earrings chimed. "It's a small industry. As I said, Atlántida is not a wealthy planet."

Her eyes swept over the ship again, lingering on the faint discoloration that mottled the off-white hull, scars left by thousands of degrees of heat and crushing kilopascals of pressure. No amount of maintenance short of a complete skin job would erase them.

"And you think this little thing is up for a long trip beyond the Rift?" she asked no one in particular.

My hands balled into fists, and my mouth opened for a potentially unwise answer.

Peter beat me to it, his voice sharp. "She's no little thing, Ma'am. *Majera's* 200 tons and a starship."

"Ah," said Sirena simply.

Peter stepped forward, pale cheeks colored pink, his muscular frame imposing under the tight, open-collared shirt. "Ma'am, *Majera's* an ex-warship. She's been scouting the starlanes for almost a hundred years and she'll last another hundred." I held back a smile. I'd never assigned a gender to my ship; the idea always seemed a little silly. Peter was more of a romantic, even if I was the one who read the trashy star romances.

"It's got a Type 3 Jump," he continued. "You won't find many ships in our class with that kind of range."

"Certainly not privately owned," Fareedh added. He had sauntered to Peter's right, a visible kind of moral support.

Peter nodded. "And as for being little, she's not. She's exactly the right size. No wasted space. Nimble. Reliable." He folded his arms. "I know every centimeter of her."

Sirena's eyebrows rose slightly. "You must be the engineer."

"You're damned right," he answered.

I smiled, remembering how it'd been like pulling gurna roots to sign Peter up in the first place. Oversized coward he might have been, but Peter could never resist an interesting physical problem or a challenge to his technical prowess.

Sirena turned to me. I quickly put my face back into a semblance of seriousness.

Her hard face softened, eyes crinkling with amusement. "I like him," she said. Then she winked.

Marta was at Peter's left now, linking her arm around his. "Me too," she said with a laugh.

I stared back at Sirena. She looked... human now. Where had the haughty princess gone?

"Darling, don't take me so seriously," she said warmly, as if reading my thoughts. "I wanted to gauge your character. I will, after all, be placing my royal personage in your hands." Her light tone belied the importance of her position.

She turned to look at Pinky. Her eyes had none of the flintiness they'd had when she'd first exchanged words with him. "I've read about your people. I knew some had come to Vatan but this... is an unexpected pleasure. Tell me, what is your role on the ship? Are you some kind of ambassador?" Her voice was almost timid.

"I plug the holes, Your Highness."

Fareedh snorted a laugh. I was mortified.

"Oh, I also navigate," he continued blithely.

Sirena blinked, nonplussed for the first time. Then she shook her head with a smile, shoulders relaxing. "You have a fine sense of humor. Yes, I think this will work out quite nicely." The princess turned to face me. "We will, of course, need to install a swimming pool, and I'd like to bring Consuelo," she said with a look to her companion. The purple-robed woman had not said a thing the whole time. "I don't know what I'd do without her," she added.

Words failed me. Things were moving so fast. All of a sudden we *had* the job? And now she was talking about a pool? And an extra passenger on top of that?

"That'd put a bit of a strain on our systems," I managed and looked towards Marta. "Wouldn't it?"

She shrugged her shoulders, her right hand absently tousling Peter's white-blond hair. "*Majera's* rated for eight crew; ten, in a pinch."

"But a *swimming pool*?" I exclaimed.

"Depends on how big it needs to be," Peter said, looking beyond Sirena, his mind at work. "We could convert the 'shop,' add double-walls, move some of the tools to our room."

Marta's frown indicated what she thought of that idea.

"Modifications to the ship would be included in the cost of the retainer," Fareedh added smoothly.

"I said that Atlántida is a poor planet," Sirena began. Her lips parted, bright teeth gleaming. "But the royal house of Atlántida shall not stint. We shall pay what needs to be paid. I trust the ship is armed?"

"Er, no," I said, slowly regaining my composure. "We're not even licensed to carry ordnance."

"We'll have to fix that," the princess said briskly. "I've heard the stories. Pirates and all that."

Peter looked at me, a little of the old fear widening his eyes. "There are pirates? I hadn't heard about pirates."

"Dead. Men. Tell. No. Tales," Pinky intoned, his voice now a deep bass.

"Precisely," Sirena said, swiveling her chair to face him. "We'll need a gun," she said with a glance at her aide. "Don't worry. Consuelo can help you with the details. She's quite good at navigating bureaucracy. Now then."

She raised her chair gracefully and floated forward. A set of bracelets tinkled at her wrist. Close up, I saw that her bare arms had a glossy sheen to them. Rather than clasping my hand, she hooked elbows, her thin arm linked with mine. "Is it a deal?"

Just like that. And I thought *I* was impetuous. This certainly wasn't what I'd expected to be doing on our first paid contract. Yet, wasn't it everything I'd ever wanted to do, all in one neat package? How could I say no? I suddenly felt giddy with a rush of excitement.

"It's a deal," I heard myself say.

Chapter 2

Launch +9 days

The hot breeze from Dayside tugged at my *tuulitakki*, the thin jacket everyone wore on Punainen as protection from the gusty, unceasing winds. Dark goggles shielded my eyes both from the driving grit and from the giant red sun, looming on the horizon several times bigger than Yeni Izmir as seen from Vatan. The goggles muted the already drab scenery. Wind erosion had flattened all natural obstacles, leaving a dusty plain dotted with hardy plants. They had broad, dark leaves low to the ground, parallel to the wind. A low shimmering rectangle, five kilometers behind me, was the windbreak that shielded much of the nearby city. It was the only notable feature besides the sun in the landscape.

Even to my wanderlusty heart, Punainen was a disappointment.

As it was, I was at the most interesting point on the planet, at the twilight zone between permanent day and night. Punainen hugged its feeble star close and had stopped spinning long ago, one face of the world permanently locked toward the star. Temperatures on Punainen's Dayside hover around a sweltering 320 degrees K. Darkside is an expanse of ice.

The ice is why people are on Punainen at all. All of that water means an easy source of fuel: the heavy isotopes of hydrogen that power the fusion reactors of the Empire's starships. Fuel that was heavily in demand once Punainen became one of the two main Cis-Rift departure points. There wasn't much else to attract Punainen's population of a few million, in settlements bathed in eternal sunset on the edge of a frosty ocean. The place had been kind of pretty at first; now it was just depressing. I was anxious to leave.

There were still two days to go before the Trans-Rift ferry left for

Hyvilma, plenty of time to top off our tanks and replenish supplies. It would take us a week to cross the Rift, the starless gap of space nearly 20 light years across that cut like a river through this part of the galaxy. Until the Type 5 Jump had been invented, capable of spanning five parsecs in a single hyperspace leap, the Rift had been a natural border for the Empire. Now there was a route across. Our ship would be shrouded in opaque handling gel and antigravved into place between containers of grain and giant pieces of a prefab factory, just one piece of cargo amongst hundreds, with us inside waiting out the ride to the first new frontier in centuries.

As it was, we would be privileged passengers. Of the thousand or so people making the trip, only a handful would travel in their own ships, most without Drives, none with *Majera's* range. The other travelers were put into cold sleep chambers; it was a lot cheaper than having to feed and sustain them for the week-long trip. Besides, hardly anyone died coming out of stasis anymore.

I sat down cross-legged and took a handful of the pink soil, let it sift from my hands in a cloud. I felt like *I* was in stasis. Ten weeks of prep and travel, another week of travel followed by more prep followed by at least *another* week of travel. The excitement I'd had when we'd left Vatan had long since worn off. All that was left was the worry that we'd miss out on a good planet.

The road to adventure is paved with planning. Lots and lots of planning, I reminded myself. Freshta Ansari's first trek to Alpha Centauri had taken six long months, bouncing from Oort Belt iceball to Oort Belt iceball, cracking her own fuel to feed an enormous Type 0 Jump. The ten weeks we had taken to get here was actually very good progress, all things considered.

There's this idea that spaceships are like cars; one just takes off when one feels like it and heads for the stars. That's how it is in a lot of books. It's what *I'd* thought when I was a kid.

The truth is a lot less romantic. Even with my old glider, I ran through a half-hour checklist before every flight. That didn't touch the maintenance of the craft—lights, airframe, *sayar*—the annual safety inspections, etc. etc. And the sailplane didn't even have an engine.

Majera was a starship. A *Yarshihar*-class Scout, it was one of the simplest, smallest, most reliable ships ever built, yet it required a hundred times more preparation than my glider. Sirena's hiring us may have been a rushed affair, but preparation could be anything but. We'd only made the one trip when Sirena had hired us, logged less than a month of shipboard time and two Jumps. Even with that little use, it *still* took us 32 Vatanian days, nearly 8 standard weeks, to get ready for this trip.

Peter had to inspect everything from top to bottom ("stem to stern" he called it). Fareedh gave our ship's *sayar* another code audit; considering what had happened last time, it made sense. Marta swapped out the filters, got food and water, tweaked the living and non-living components of the air system. Peter may have the title of "engineer," but I saw tools in Marta's hands just as often, and the stuff she worked with was a lot more disgusting.

Pinky and I helped with the additions. The "pool" ended up pretty small — about three meters on a side — but it still added a troubling 20 tons to our mass. Figuring out how to trim the ship to compensate for the imbalance had given Peter and Fareedh an extra set of headaches.

It was all necessary work. Nevertheless, each day we spent in preparation was another day some other team might be claiming the best spot on a likely Trans-Rift planet — or even the whole world.

We'd launched at last on the 46th of Dust, the ugliest of Vatan's nine months. The capital city of Denizli had been a blur of skyscrapers amidst the ruddy fuzz of diffuse pollen blown in from the vast plains of the north. I was glad to be getting away, tired of having to wear a mask outdoors. We floated up from the planet on antigravity like a balloon and were a safe distance from Vatan within a couple of hours. *Majera* slid into hyperspace without incident.

What a difference from last time.

In fact, the Jump from Vatan to Punainen, was… odd, subdued. I've known Pinky, Marta, and Peter forever, and though Fareedh was a relative newcomer to our group, the last flight had solidified his friendship with all of us. We were all very comfortable with each other. A unit. No — a crew.

But now that we were under contract, and with *royalty* on board, for Lord's sake, things were somehow tense. We didn't see Consuelo, and Sirena hardly left the room with the pool, which was also her and

Consuelo's living quarters.

So I'd gotten a lot of reading done, played a few games with Pinky, did a couple of practice runs on the bridge to get myself familiar with Punainen's navigation protocols. That was pretty much it. Again, reality doesn't live up to fiction: space travel can be pretty boring. I'd looked forward to our reentering normal space, to seeing what Punainen had to offer. After all, it was on the edge of the Frontier, and it was a world I had never visited, or if I had, it was too long ago to remember. After the week-long trip, we'd Jumped out right into the inbound traffic lane, the volume of space reserved for arrivals on that day and hour, and headed toward Punainen's orbital starport.

And now here I was, wearing a mask and dealing with dust. I could have stayed home.

I rubbed the fingers of my right hand together and thought about going back to the ship, idly looking around for a suitable rock to add to my collection of off-world specimens.

A flicker of motion behind me got my attention. I looked over my shoulder and saw Sirena Isabella de Atlántida Jáimez VII gliding toward me, her lower half hidden in the conical shell of her grav chair. She wore a transparent jacket over a green sleeveless dress, a shimmering shawl in her lap. Even through my goggles, the colors were riotous. I sprang to my feet before I was aware I was doing it.

"Are you always so jumpy?" the princess called out.

I looked down, noticed I was standing, and tried to relax. "Sorry, Your Highness."

She ran her fingers through flame red hair and gave me a dazzling smile.

"Sirena is fine, darling."

"Yes, Your Highne... Sirena." I put a hand on my hip and affected a slouch, trying to remember how Fareedh always made the gesture look so casual and compelling. "I can't help it. It's how I was raised."

The princess floated closer, lowering her chair to just a few centimeters off the ground. "Please sit. I am." Her eyes danced. I noted she wasn't wearing goggles.

I sat, hugging my knees. Somehow I felt compelled to explain myself. "You're royalty," I said. This close, I didn't have to raise my voice much to be heard over the wind.

"Just planetary royalty," she replied.

I snorted. "'Just.'"

"You Imperials take titles too seriously."

My eyebrow quirked. "Atlántida is Imperial."

She dismissed the point with a wave of her thin hand. "Mid-worlds are a little less in awe of the Imperial system."

I nodded to show that I understood, though I didn't necessarily agree with the sentiment. Vatan, like the other planets at the edge of the settled Frontier, had only been colonized 150 years before, mostly by Core-world stock using new, faster ships. The colonies of the Mid-worlds were a lot different, from us, and from each other. Six hundred years ago, when the first ships left Earth, their crude Jump drives capable of barely three light years of range, every colonization effort had been a gamble. Most of the Mid-worlds had followed their own path for centuries before Jump drives got good enough to knit the Empire together with travel times measured in weeks instead of months.

"It's not just that," I tried to explain. "My mother was an ambassador. I can't tell you how many fêtes and parades I attended as a kid. I still know the order of precedence for every noble, from the Empress to the third child of the Baron of Fornax."

Sirena pondered for a moment, then slid a heavy ring off one of her slim fingers. She tucked it into a pocket of her chair that appeared only when she touched it and disappeared when her hand had left it.

"There," she said. "No more princess. Just me."

I let out a breath. "That does help," I said. "How did you find me, anyway?"

Sirena laughed, a silver sound that rose above the rush of the wind. "A lone figure at the edge of the world? It wasn't hard. And Fareedh told me you'd gone exploring."

"Yeah. I saw most of the city the first day. Not too exciting. Just the Kader Museum."

Aside from its position, Punainen's main claim to fame was having been the birthplace of Helmi Kader, who a few years back had discovered remains of an apparently long dead intelligent alien society. That had increased the total known number of alien civilizations, living or dead, to four, and Kader had entered the history books. And, truth to tell, my heart. Marta, back when she'd been my girlfriend, had been remarkably patient during my celebrity crush phase that had lasted a good half of Third Year. I was over it now. Mostly.

Which was just as well. There hadn't been much to the Museum. Helmi had left Punainen as a teenager almost 20 years ago, and all of her important work had been done on Syr Darya, the homeworld or colony of the extinct aliens.

Sirena nodded. "Not much opportunity for nightlife on a planet with no night." Her smile faded and she looked at me earnestly, "Kitra, I need your help."

My eyes widened. I hadn't expected that.

"It's Consuelo. I don't think I can bring her with me," she went on. The ochre skin of Sirena's face, already lighter after the week in hyperspace, was positively pale.

"What's wrong?"

"She just doesn't have the, how do you say, constitution for this. Hyperspace, it gnaws at her. She doesn't eat, and she has difficulty sleeping."

"Jump sickness." It wasn't too common, maybe one in a hundred got it. "There are pills," I suggested.

Sirena shook her head. "It goes beyond that. Consuelo won't admit it, but she needs solid ground. Structure. She's a creature of civilization." Sirena passed the back of her hand across her forehead. "Oh, I don't know what I was thinking dragging her along. It's just, I've never been without her."

I nodded again. I wasn't sure what to say.

She looked at me searchingly. "What do you think of Consuelo?"

I opened my mouth, paused and pursed my lips. What *did* I think of Consuelo? She wasn't much for conversation. At first, I thought it was because her French was almost non-existent, but Marta spoke Spanish, and she didn't get much out of her either. I'd only really had one interaction with her, and it wasn't entirely positive.

"She's pretty brilliant," I said. "We wouldn't have the gun without her." I meant it to sound like praise, but my emphasis on the word 'gun' changed the tone of the sentence.

"It's not really a gun," Sirena noted.

That was true. Technically, it was a communications laser with restricted power and frequencies. It was the only thing we could get licensed and installed in the time we had. It wasn't even that expensive: we were able to use the pricy capacitors that had come with the ship. But even if comms were the official use, you can do a lot of damage with a focused, high energy stream of photons.

"Close enough."

"You sound like you're not happy about it," Sirena said.

I licked my lips. "I understand why we have one, and why you insisted on it. I just... I don't like guns."

"Why not?"

I took a deep breath and decided to be honest. It had been bothering me for weeks.

"It's the principle. My mom was a diplomat. Her motto was 'there is always a peaceful solution.' A gun, especially something that can take apart a ship at range... it just doesn't sit right with me."

I suppressed a shudder. Ships were fragile things, something I knew all too well after what had happened long ago to me and my parents. Sirena looked down at the rim of her chair where the arc of silver met the shawl covering the lower half of her body. "Consuelo can be a bit overprotective." She chuckled. "It's been like that since I was a child. You can imagine how deadset she was against my coming out here. Especially without an armed escort."

"How did you convince her?"

She looked up at me, her eyes flashing. "I *am* a princess, you know." Her expression softened. "A very minor one. Headstrong enough to get my way, unimportant enough to be expendable. It made more sense to travel to Vatan incognito rather than making a big show of it, though I can't imagine I'd fetch much ransom if I were kidnapped."

The idea of nobility traveling around in disguise was like something from a story, but it was completely possible in a universe where news didn't travel between planets any faster than people. It took weeks for mail ships to carry messages from star to star, but it took light waves years to travel the same distance.

"I have to say, it's all been very exciting," Sirena went on. "After years of being cloistered in palaces, it's lovely to go to the stars rather than simply observe them. Of course, all of the places I've seen have been settled worlds. I won't be completely satisfied until I've been to

17

a system no one has visited before."

"But Consuelo has Jump sickness," I said.

"Consuelo has Jump sickness."

"Which means you can't go?"

She raised her eyebrows in a shrug, looking to the side. "It means she can't go. And I have a decision to make."

"Whether to go on without her."

"That's it on an oyster shell, yes."

I made a noncommittal sound, a little laugh, and Sirena nodded ruefully as if I'd said something very wise. We both looked down. The wind continued to blow, an unending muted roar, sometimes accompanied by the hiss of traveling soil.

The princess ran a hand through her hair, and it went streaming behind her like a comet. She smiled when I looked up. "Of course, I can't imagine this trip will be as eventful as your last one," she said. We'd filled her in on the details of our first jaunt. She'd insisted, and of course, it wouldn't have been honest to leave her in the dark.

"Hopefully. Provided our ship's *sayar* is working like it should."

Her eyes went round. "Gracious, darling," She pursed her lips in thought and asked. "We couldn't have another mis-Jump, could we?"

I shouldn't have teased her. I looked up at her with what I hoped was a reassuring smile. "Oh no. Like I said, Fareedh's been through the code a dozen times now."

"That's good," she said, visibly relaxing. She tapped my knee conspiratorially. "He really is a handsome man, isn't he?"

I blinked. "Um, sure?" I mean, he *was*, but I hadn't expected that to come up, certainly not with Sirena.

She shook her head, as if in wonder. "You led them through all that happened. The mis-Jump, the refueling, everything. Despite it all, you got the ship home."

"It was a team effort," I insisted, but I looked away from her penetrating gaze. "None of us could have done it without each other."

Sirena leaned forward with her chin in her hand, pondering. I noticed the slight webbing of skin between each of her fingers. I'd had a friend in high school who had been born with similar hands. It had made it harder for him to play stringed instruments, but he was also a star water-ball athlete. According to Sirena, all of her family, and many on Atlántida had hands like hers, though Consuelo did not.

"What are you thinking about?" I asked.

"About all you had to go through. You packed more into one jaunt than most do in a dozen." She coughed out a small laugh. "Or I do in a lifetime."

"Are you rethinking your decision?" It occurred to me that she might give up on us and find another crew, one whose missions hadn't been a series of mishaps.

"Don't be silly, darling. I've no illusions that this will be a, how you say, 'flight to the moon'. I'm glad to know all the things that could go wrong."

"I'm sure it's not a full list!" I laughed.

"No, but it is representative." She smoothed her shawl with her left hand. "I think I've solved my Consuelo problem."

"You have?"

"Yes. I know that a trip beyond the Frontier will be no good for her. And I know that even without her, I still have someone I can completely count on." Sirena looked at me meaningfully and put her hand lightly on my shoulder. "I know I've got the right team. The right captain."

I felt my cheeks flush.

"I'll try not... I won't let you down, Your Highness."

"Sirena," she said, smiling as she put her hands back in her lap.

"Sirena," I repeated.

19

Chapter 3

The Hotel Hyvilma was done in rustic style, playing into the city's role as capital of the biggest Trans-Frontier colony. The native equivalent of wood paneled the walls. There was even a giant fireplace in the middle of the lounge, though I hadn't checked to see if it was virtual or not. It was all very cozy.

In the 15 minutes since I'd sat down, two big groups had filed through the lobby toward reception. Hyvilma was a busy planet. What I'd seen of it on my way from the spaceport suggested an orderly downtown surrounded by rings of ramshackle chaos, like a tree that had grown too fast. It was kind of charming, vibrant after the sleepy maturity of Vatan and the monotony of Punainen. Hyvilma's cheery yellow sun, hot and small in the sky, seemed brighter than Yeni Izmir.

In fact, everything felt more intense, all of my senses extra sensitive. Perhaps it was the contrast to the dull week we'd spent in transit. Maybe it was the excitement of finally being Trans-Rift. The breakfast smells were exotic: oatmeal, rye bread, fried eggs, and coffee. There was no Turkish coffee to be had, at least that I'd found in my limited exploration, but there was no shortage of the brew in its more conventional form. I sipped at a mug, the temperature of its contents appropriately scalding. Light and full flavored, it didn't taste like it had come out of a Maker. That made sense. The hotel even had human staff, so I didn't think they'd skimp on food.

Fareedh's lanky form became visible through the fog above my mug. He was smiling mischievously, hands behind his back. With my high-keyed senses, the sharp lines of his face seemed extra dramatic, the dark tone of his skin particularly warm and appealing. Sirena was right. He *was* a handsome guy.

"Good morning," he said. "You look content."

I cradled my mug possessively. "I got my coffee. Plus I like that the day here is close to Standard. Getting up with the sunrise was nice." The double-long days on Vatan meant one alternated waking up in light and darkness. I'd grown up with it my whole life, but there was something natural about following the sun.

He shrugged, still smiling. "I kind of like the variation back home. By the way, I've got something for you." He held out his hand, in which was a small plastic box.

The plush chairs in the hotel lounge gave back rubs. I was a little reluctant to get up, but I managed it.

"What is it?" I asked automatically. Dumb question. There was an easy way to find out. To Fareedh's credit, he didn't point that out. He simply took one of my hands and put the box in it.

"Thanks," I said. My fingers slid over the slick brown surface. "Do I open it here?"

"You can if you want. It's nothing special."

I smiled and thumbed open the container. The top slid aside revealing something round and gray. It was symmetrical, smooth, but with a subtle spiral relief to it, like a tattoo. Touching it, it felt like stone.

"A rock? No... a fossil of some kind?"

Fareedh nodded, his adorable poof of black hair wobbling slightly. "I know you're into souvenirs, and I figured you'd want something that couldn't come out of a Maker. It's from the coastal strip, maybe ten million years old." He smiled, his teeth gleaming. "At least, that's what the person who sold it to me said. What do I know about rocks?"

I touched the little gift, perhaps three centimeters in diameter. An alien creature that had lived its whole life long before there were humans, before there were even upright apes. Unlike Punainen and even Vatan, Hyvilma had an advanced ecosystem when people discovered it. This stone shell was just one tiny example of it. It was exactly the kind of gift I liked, inexpensive but priceless. And tailored for me.

"I love it," I said, returning Fareedh's smile as I sat back down. I didn't have a bag or pockets to put the fossil in, so I placed it in my lap so I wouldn't forget it. I gestured to one of the chairs around the low table crafted from Hyvilman lumber. "Care to join me?"

"Gladly." He set himself into the chair in his usual unorthodox way, legs folded and crossed under him. He was wearing short pants under his swirly blue shirt, little black hairs curled over his skinny limbs. "Is it just us?"

"For now," I said with a nod. "I'm sure they'll be up soon, though."

"Like old times." He meant when we'd met at Erkki's back in Denizli, the time I'd broken the news that I'd bought *Majera*.

"I guess it is, isn't it? Except this time I don't have to sell you and the rest on this trip."

He leaned back and looked at the vaulted ceiling. "As I recall, I didn't take much convincing."

"Not quite as much as Peter, no…"

"Touché. Well, I'm not sorry you convinced me."

I took another pull of coffee, wanting it in me before it got cold. Fareedh sat upright suddenly. "Oh, did I tell you I got to talk to my brother last night?"

I knew he had a younger sister. I barely remembered he had a brother. I'd never met him.

"Oh yeah? How's ol' what's-his-name doing?"

He laughed. "His name's Iskender. Still in the Navy."

"Is he on base?" I knew the Empire maintained a facility on Hyvilma, separate from the civilian starport.

Fareedh shook his head. "He's a Lieutenant on the *Faucon*. It's too big to land. I didn't actually see him. We just talked over the *sayar*."

"How's he doing?"

"About the same. He drew about the luckiest assignment you can get. Trans-Rift, away from the Mid-world unrest spots or the Grilchie wars. On a cruiser rather than a corvette so he's not chasing pirates. Standard 'show the flag' duty. I don't think he's complaining."

I brushed my hair back and took a last swallow of coffee. "If he's anything like you, it'd take a lot to make him complain."

Fareedh shrugged easily. "He's a *little* more ambitious than me. But he's happy right now. He figures he's got another year or two, and then — "

Marta's voice, high and musical, sounded from across the lobby, "Good morning!" Fareedh and I, and about half a dozen other break-fasting hotel guests, turned. And not just because she'd attracted at-tention with her voice. She and Peter walked toward us, arms linked. As always, they made an impressive pair: Peter bulky in a tight-fitting matched set of light shirt and trousers, Marta all height and broad curves in a velvety dress. I looked self-consciously at my baggy shirt and knee-length stretch pants, then caught Fareedh catching me. He shrugged his eyebrows, silently conveying that he knew he was also part of the schlub club. To be fair, Peter hadn't dressed up before he started going out with Marta. That was part of the reason Marta and I weren't dating anymore; I'd never had much fashion sense, no matter how hard Marta tried to instill some in me.

"This place is pretty rich," Peter said when he got to our table. "I'm not used to my favorites being on the main menu, much less all-you-can-eat." Hyvilma had been settled mostly by Finnish Mid-worlders, like Peter and Marta's ancestors. Vatan was pure Core-world, mostly Turkish and French in culture and cuisine. Peter had always complained that he had to go home to get good food.

He looked down at the empty spot of table in front of Fareedh then up at him. "You haven't gotten anything yet?"

"I just arrived," Fareedh murmured.

"Oh, man. Let's go check out the food."

Marta put a restraining hand on his shoulder. "Hold on. I want to give the present first."

I felt my eyebrows go up. "Present?"

Marta nodded with a bright grin. "Just a little something." She started digging around the stylish little bag slung over her shoulder.

"From both of us," Peter added quickly.

"Yes, here it is." It was a little square thing, coated in red and white wrapping foil. She leaned over and pressed it into my hands.

This time, I didn't ask what it was. "Thanks," I said. "You want me to open it now?"

"The sooner you do, the sooner we eat," Peter said. Marta el-bowed him gently.

It turned out the wrapping was ephemeral, the kind that flickers away when the package is opened. Inside was… a little gray fossil, a virtual twin to the other one I'd gotten. I glanced up at Fareedh uneasily, but he just looked amused.

"I know you like rocks for the Specimen Table," Marta was saying, "and it seemed like something that had once been alive would be even more special." She looked expectantly at me.

"It's... amazing, you two." I forced my smile to broaden. "You definitely know me."

Peter nodded smugly at Marta while I spread my thighs just enough for Fareedh's box to drop out of sight. I gave the new box pride of place on the table. Marta looked expectantly at me. I knew that expression—she was waiting for a hug. How could I get up without Fareedh's gift tumbling to the floor?

Peter saved me. "Now can we get breakfast?" he asked, half turned toward the serving station. Marta inclined her head toward him and nodded.

"Wait! We can't eat yet." Pinky's voice rumbled from behind my two standing friends. Peter groaned, but he stepped aside to give him a clear path to the table. Pinky was a shockingly hot pink, clearly excited about something. He strode on two legs toward the table, two of his three arms folded behind his... well, not his back, but the side opposite from me. Behind him I noticed that folks at their tables had lowered their voices, stealing glances at what was probably their first sight of an alien.

"Sorry I'm late. I was getting your present ready."

I swallowed. "Present?" My voice was a squeak, so I coughed and repeated the word.

Pinky pulsed purple a couple of times, his version of a nod when he forgot to mimic human gestures.

"Of course. I found the perfect thing for you. The gift that says 'I've been your best friend since childhood and know you better than anyone.' Something to display in your cabin with pride."

Marta looked at me, a quizzical look on her face. Then she glanced at Fareedh, who was *also* looking at me.

Before I could say anything, Pinky was speaking again. "Here you go! A souvenir of Hyvilma just for you." His thick, rubbery arms had rotated to his front. In one clumsy, three-fingered hand was a small gray box.

"Oh!" I exclaimed with mock surprise. "You got me a fossil! That's perfect."

Pinky went maroon with puzzlement. "A fossil? Why would I get you that?"

"I... uh... no reason. 'What did you get me?' I meant."

He opened the box with a flourish and plucked out an iridescent little ellipsoid. This he tossed onto the broad table with a flourish. In a blink, the capsule was gone and so was the table. In its place was a holo of a landscape, three brown pyramids against a shimmering yellow horizon. I recognized the place, *Kolme Veljeä*, one of the planet's most prominent natural features. It was a triplet of mountains just visible from the edge of the capital. I'd seen them on the way down from orbit, but they looked particularly striking captured at sunrise, as they were in the holo.

The beauty of the shot was somewhat marred by the garish lettering across the sky above the peaks spelling out in French, "HYVILMA: YOUR GATEWAY TO THE UNKNOWN!"

I looked up at Pinky. "A wall sprawl?" I asked.

"Just something to remember this place by."

"It's... nice," I said. "Thanks."

"No, no. You missed the best part!" Pinky said, pointing toward the rim of the table closest to me. The sprawl spread over the edge, tilting perpendicular toward the floor. I put a palm where I'd seen the ellipsoid last, found it, and pushed it away from me. The rest of the holo came into view, including a round figure in silhouette. It was obviously Pinky, standing on three legs with two spindly arms stretched out a full meter on either side. There were two fingers apiece on the outstretched hands, spread in a "V", the typical tourist holo pose.

Underneath the figure were more words: "Two natural treasures for the price of one!" and next to them, in very small print, "Not actually a product of the Hyvliman Matkailutoimisto (Tourism Bureau)."

"I'll treasure it always," I said flatly. But the upward quirk of my lips betrayed me. It was pretty funny. "That's what you were doing this morning?"

Pinky gave a very human shrug with two of his shoulders. "I could have used my *sayar* to edit myself into a commercial sprawl, but I wanted it to be authentic. And to include Hyvilma's current best feature. Me."

Fareedh nodded in appreciation. "Nicely done," he said.

"It's alright," Pinky said, his humble tone belied by a momentary deep flush of his skin. His eyespots turned to me. "Do you really like it? Should I have gotten you a fossil instead?"

"No," I said quickly. "This is just perfect."

"Why a fossil?" Marta asked. The question may have been to Pinky, but she was looking right at me. No, into my lap where Fareedh's small box laid half obscured. With a sheepish grin, I put it on the table next to hers and tapped it open. They were not only the same species, but it was clear both fossils had been gotten at the same shop.

"Oh," Marta said, her features darkening. "Maybe I could return it..."

"No," Fareedh interjected, "I can take mine back."

I put a hand possessively on each of the fossils. "Don't you dare break up my matched set." I smiled at Marta and Fareedh in turn. "If a gift is perfect, then two of that gift is twice as perfect." It was easy to say the words with sincerity. It was actually pretty neat having a pair of fossils for the table rather than just one.

And to prove I was serious, I got up and gave everyone hugs, saving Marta for last. Her return squeeze left me a bit winded.

Sirena's voice lilted through the growing sounds of the breakfast crowd. "Such a close-knit crew. That bodes well for our journey." She glided toward us, dressed modestly, for her, in a silvery chemise that looked classy but not too formal or rich. Sensible. Hyvilma was still a solidly well-policed Imperial world, but it was wise not to advertise one's wealth or position too much. "Since we're all here," she said, "why don't we get some breakfast, and then let's get down to business?"

Peter was already halfway to the food counters by the time she finished the sentence.

"I still like the idea of heading toward Kochab," Sirena was saying, her tone insistent. "If anything, it's poetic."

The wreckage of six meals laid strewn across the table, and several floating *sayar* displays competed for space above: star charts, spectrograms, fuel consumption curves. On this side of the Rift, systems fanned out thickly as far as the telescope could see, almost one every parsec. We still hadn't chosen our destination from among them. The problem was, public surveys only included the stars closest to Hyvilma. Beyond that, it was just astronomy and guesswork. The wrong guess could leave us light years from home without an easy way back, and at the very least, each time we went out without finding a suitable planet was another stretch of weeks someone else might beat us to a claim.

I studied Sirena's display: Kochab was a fiercely luminous orange dot in the holo of stars above her *sayar*. A giant star at the end of its lifespan, it was easily the brightest star in the Hyvilman sky, visible even in the daytime if one knew where to look. I'd read that it could be seen all the way from old Earth and that its name predated starflight. From Hyvilma, it was just five parsecs away — the light captured in Sirena's holo was only 16 years old.

"Poetry aside," Fareedh countered, "the choices are few in that direction." He turned his display into a color coded position map, blanked out everyone else's, and pointed to a red star two parsecs from Hyvilma. "This is GM 71. Nothing here except a gas giant and a couple of burned out rocks. The Navy's got a base, and they'll sell fuel at a premium, but that's it. And then beyond that is GM 191." His finger slid to a yellow sun just beyond safe Jump range from Hyvilma. "There are three colonies on the system's one inhabitable planet, mostly folks from Syr Darya." That was the other Cis-Rift port besides Punainen.

"Yes, but beyond there is a whole wealth of possibilities," Sirena insisted, "Right Pinky?"

Pinky extended a finger to twice the length of Fareedh's. "Technically. Beyond 191 is Kochab this way, a planetless red star that way. But these three worlds here..." He waggled the overlong digit at a cluster of stars so close to each other that they might have been a system with a common origin. One was a bright yellow sun blazing away by itself. The other six were all red, in pairs.

Marta leaned forward and poked at the system Pinky had called planetless. A pair of miniature displays came to life. One showed a smooth sine wave, the radial velocity — the speed of the star's movement with respect to Hyvilma. Had there been any planets of size, the graph would have wobbles in it: the gravitational tugging of the planets as they went around their star. The other display was a light curve graphing the star's light over time. It was flat, which meant no telltale dimming as planets crossed in front of the star in their orbits — more evidence that there was nothing to explore there.

Those graphs were absent when Marta cycled through the displays of the four systems at the end of Pinky's finger. "This is the best we can get, huh?" she said. "There's no long term data at all."

"These are from the big survey three years ago," Pinky said. "They brought in a couple of giant 'scopes just for the job. If we want to know more, we'll have to head out Kochab way and get the info ourselves."

"I can't believe no one's done that yet," Sirena said dubiously. "The Frontier's been open for decades now."

"Maybe the Navy has and they just aren't telling anyone," Peter said.

"And there haven't been a lot of private ships with our range on this side of the Frontier," I pointed out with pride. "Even fewer, the further back you go." I stared hard at the four mystery systems with seven suns between them, as if I might get some kind of premonition about them. No such luck. "All right," I said. "Pinky, can you go over the other path again?"

He slowly extruded a third arm and gripped at Fareedh's floating map. "If I may?" he asked, rotating the display toward him. "The first star in this direction is Son Duryak, this orange star over here about two parsecs out." He spread two long fingers and the display zoomed in to reveal a stylized set of orbital ellipses. "Planet Three is kind of a dud, mostly airless but with vast ice fields. There are no real colonies here yet, but several areas have been staked out and there are a couple of automated fuel refineries set up with a few people staffing them. They service the outgoing survey and colony ships."

Peter frowned. "Everyone and their mother would be going that way," he said.

I zoomed the display out again. Space is really big, and it goes in three dimensions; there had to be more than just two options. I found a red star midway in direction between Kochab and Son Duryak. The displays above it indicated that there was water to be had, and it was three parsecs away, at the extreme limit of our range. That suggested it wouldn't be visited as often. "Why wouldn't we go, say, here?"

"It's interdicted," Pinky explained.

"Quarantined?" Marta asked. "Why? By who?"

The alien spread all three arms out in a shrug. "By the Navy, and who knows why? Anyway, Son Duryak's not as well-trodden as you think. It mostly serves as a stepping stone to these five stars around it, all of them within two parsecs; that's the maximum range of virtually all civilian ships this side of the Rift. *These* are the candidates I'm looking at."

Another jab of his finger, and there were range lines sprouting from Son Duryak to two orange stars, both at the extreme range that *Majera* could Jump from Son Duryak and each other. Orbits, radial velocity curves, and spectrographs popped up, too. "GM 106 and 107," he said. "They've both got a couple of gas giants and a few terrestrial worlds."

"Hmmm." Marta pursed her lips, paging through several screens on her *sayar*. "107's a younger system, it looks like, from the X-ray signature and the dust halo."

"It's got two planets orbiting in the water zone," Fareedh pointed out. "Not too hot, not too cold."

"That doesn't mean there's any liquid water, though. We can't even be sure of the mass of those planets. There's only radial velocity data to go on—no eclipses in the light curve data." Marta twirled her manicured fingers, cycling to other displays. The ones dealing with GM 106 grew and glowed brighter. "Number Two in this one looks pretty good," she said after a quick perusal. "There's eclipse data and even some spectrographs of the planet's atmosphere. Looks like water *and* oxygen in the spectrum. Plus, we know its mass. Definitely terrestrial," she finished.

It took a moment for it to register that no one was following her with anything to say. When I looked up, everyone was looking expectantly at me.

"Oh, you want *me* to make the decision," I said.

"You are the captain," Fareedh said simply.

I looked over at Sirena. She had argued so strongly for Kochab that I was hesitant to suggest anything else. But she smiled gently and nodded.

I considered the map. Both directions promised some kind of pay-off at the end of two Jumps. Kochab way was more of a mystery, but because of that, less likely to have been explored. On the other hand, I'd done the blind Jump thing before, and it hadn't been fun. Better a bird in the hand than two on a branch. It made sense to go to the one system we knew would have fuel for us at the end of a long Jump.

"Let's do 106," I said.

Chapter 4

Coming out of hyperspace, or going in, for that matter, is never pleasant. Whatever weird dimensions exist in the space between space, they don't seem to like being penetrated by things from normal space. The ships handle it well enough; there are power fields that prevent too much physical strain on the hull.

People, on the other hand, have no such luxury. I laid slumped in my crash couch, hands on the control sticks, feeling the cramps and nausea slowly subsiding. It was like a bad period, at least from what I remembered of them; I hadn't had to deal with one since I was 16 and old enough for the shot.

Pinky asked, "Rough transition?"

"No worse than usual," I said, keeping my eyes fixed forward on the Window. The virtual display that spanned most of the front of the bridge had just snapped on, revealing an expanse of stars.

"There's pills, you know," Fareedh's voice came from behind me, tinged with a smile.

"Not for our fearless leader," Peter said. A year ago, that would have been a sarcastic jab, but he said it straight this time. It was flattering. I probably should have taken pills, though.

My grip on the sticks tightened as I strained my ears for a collision alarm. It hadn't sounded on any of my previous jumps, and there was even less chance of it here in the vicinity of GM 106 #2, where there wasn't supposed to be any space traffic. But there's always a first time. A drop of sweat rolled down my neck.

Navigating a Jump of several light years meant taking into account the relative positions and velocities of destination and target, not to mention a lot of uncertainties which, when you added up all the margins of error, could easily prove lethal. If your Jump-out point was too close to a planet, you might never leave hyperspace. Pop into normal space at the crowded end of a shipping lane, and you might find your hull merged with that of another vessel... explosively.

The ship's *sayar* did a lot of the work, but it could only offer suggestions, provide probability maps with margins of error. In the end, it took a living brain with a strong grasp of hyperdimensional mathematics to plot courses between stars, to make educated decisions on where to enter and exit Jump safely so as to minimize the danger of collision and usage of fuel. I always found it ironic that Pinky should be so good at interstellar navigation given that his people hadn't even known about the stars until humans descended through their planet's permanent overcast decades ago.

But no alarm sounded. A good first sign. *Majera* looked healthy, too. 'The Tree' — the branching constellation of lights below the Window showing the status of *Majera's* systems — was all green. Greener than ever. On the last trip, I'd gotten used to two of its lights remaining an inactive brown: the multi-use pod and the weapons pod. The latter indicator now glowed serenely at me. The other floating displays, showing our fuel level, ship systems status, and a myriad of other useful information, all reported nominal conditions. There were no hazards on the close proximity sensors.

We were fine. Now I just needed to know where we were.

"How're we looking?" I asked tightly.

"With eyespots, Kitra."

I slowly turned my head towards Pinky and waited.

"Oh, you mean our position," he said casually. The Window's vantage shifted and the crescent arc of a planet rose into view. He raised three arms expansively. "Right on the button. Voilà."

It was a lovely view. Beyond the crescent world, the orange disk of a star blazed off to the right, the ship's display filtering it to a tolerable brightness. From its apparent size and what I knew about it, it was possible to estimate our distance. It was clear Pinky had done at least a fair job of navigation. We had to be pretty near to our destination, the orbit of the second planet of the system. I rolled my neck, making audible pops as the tension eased. As I watched, the sunlit portion widened, glittering almost pure white. At first I thought it might be cloud cover, but the reflection was so bright that the Window filters snapped on again. Water? No, ice.

An aristocratic soprano voice rang out, "Is that my new world, darling?" I swiveled to see Sirena gliding forward, coming to rest just behind me and Pinky, the blunted point of her chair hovering a few centimeters above the deck.

"Yes, Ma'am," Pinky said. "GM 106; Number Two."

"I hereby dub thee Glowworm," Fareedh murmured.

"Darling, I think I bought the right to name the planet," Sirena said, then winked at him. "Glowworm will serve for now. It's better than 'GM 106 Number Two." She narrowed her eyes at the vista in the Window. "Brrr," she said, hugging her bare arms close. "An ice planet doesn't seem very hospitable." The goosepimpling of her skin had to have been psychosomatic—we'd kept *Majera* a couple of degrees warmer and more humid than usual per her request.

"It's not all ice," Fareedh said. I heard his fingers tap on his panel and the planet transformed from a white and black disk to a rugged relief map in outline, all oranges and grays. He'd activated the deep radar. "The polar caps do go down pretty far, but there's a clear belt of unfrozen ocean around the planet's equator about, oh, 30 degrees wide."

"But is there any land?" the princess asked. "We don't need another water planet."

"There is," Fareedh said, "but it's all under the ice on this side. Up at the top." With that direction, I made out the contours of a small continent, its coasts sliding sharply into the basins of the oceans, close to the planet's North Pole.

"We're in a two-hour orbit," Pinky said, looking at our course plot on the panel. "We'll see the planet's back-side soon enough."

The tip of a mountainous mass slid into view over the edge of the planet far from the poles. I switched the Window back to natural light, and the mass showed up grayish-brown against the deep blue of ocean, a front of clouds curled off its southern coast. We watched in silence as the land continued its creep toward us. When blue finally appeared behind it, it was clear we'd found a small continent right on the world's equator.

"Looking good," Fareedh said, echoing all of our thoughts.

"Can we breathe the air?" Sirena asked briskly. She'd clearly moved on to the next item in her mental checklist.

Pinky popped up a display partition on the Window with the planet's spectrograph and a list of gases sorted by concentration. Molecular nitrogen was at the top with oxygen close behind. The projected surface pressure was 90 kilopascals, only a little thin.

"Are we the first ones here?" Peter asked. "That's the important question."

"I've been checking," Marta said. "No claim beacons. No signal traffic at all."

"It's perfect," I said, my grin widening as I relaxed into my seat. First-time lucky! "Cold or not, that's a good world."

"Don't count your flowers until they've bloomed," Marta said lightly. "Who knows what kind of bugs live on this planet?"

"Not to mention things bigger than bugs," Pinky added.

Fareedh chuckled. "Where's your sense of adventure?"

"In a box, and still worn-out after our last trip, thank you very much," Peter shot back. Then, in a more thoughtful tone, "Still, it's definitely worth checking out. In any event, we'll need to land if we want to fill our tanks. That's the only easy source of hydrogen for several light years. Unless Kitra wants to go giant diving again."

"Pass," I said quickly. I looked up at Sirena. She was eyeing the world keenly, as if trying to see through it.

Then she nodded. "Let's see if this planet will make a good Duchy for the House of Atlántida."

I sent *Majera* into a gentle descent toward the likeliest spot I could find: a ragged bay fringed with wild green growth. We dropped slowly, like a balloon with a slow leak. There wasn't any sensation of movement, the ship's antigrav keeping us steady at 1.1 standard gees, the weight we were used to on Vatan. It was a wasteful maneuver, fuel-use wise, but that didn't matter. The floating screen above my control panel said our tanks were 36% full. Not enough for a hyperspace Jump of more than a few light years, but there was plenty to spare for cruising around a planet, especially one with oceans of water to be cracked into hydrogen fuel.

How different from when I'd landed *Majera* on Jaiyk, gliding in on the ship's stubby wings to save gas. Like spaceships did back in the old days before antigrav.

The arc of the planet gradually flattened and became a horizon, the Window dimming the glare off the vast ice sheets in front of us. Black, starry sky slowly brightened to deep indigo, then midnight blue, like surfacing from the depths of an ocean, but in reverse.

"Anything wrong, Captain?" Sirena's voice came from behind me.

I looked up at her, not understanding.

"Your hands."

I looked down, then smiled sheepishly. I'd kept my hands on the flight sticks, my grip tight. I loosened my clutch on the controls and flexed my fingers. The ship's autopilot was certainly up to a simple job like this. I just found it hard to trust it.

Which Fareedh knew. "It's standard procedure," he said to Sirena. "You never know when a hard jet stream is going to blow across our path and maybe send us into a tumble."

I swiveled in my chair and gave him a grateful smile, to which he replied with a surreptitious wink, the kind that once would have made me blush. I was used to them now.

Sirena unfolded her bare arms. "Don't worry, darling. I'd much rather be safe than sorry. I just wanted to be sure everything was all right."

We were just fifteen kilometers up now, well within the planet's stratosphere where high winds would blow. "How about it, Fareedh? What's it like outside?" I asked.

He gave his panel a quick look. "Frosty. 253 degrees Kelvin, and wind speeds are up to 30 kph."

No worse than expected. "Thanks," I said, turning back to the Window.

Through the screen, I saw the spot I'd picked out sprawling around and below us. It looked even better from this height than it had from orbit, the big bay protected by a cape of little islands. We were low enough that I could see the contrast between the rough breakers pounding the barrier isles and the calm of the interior waters. The land was green, with forest covering the ground all the way to the shore.

"Looks like you'll have a lot more to play with than last time," Peter said to Marta. "The wardroom's going to end up a zoo again."

"You get your toys, I get mine." I could hear the smile in her voice.

With the altitude reading in the tens of meters now, I took control of the *Majera* from the ship's *sayar*. There was a nice dark patch of what looked like moss or grass over flat land. Pinky, always one step ahead of me, flipped on the deep radar, transforming greens and blues and soft edges into a stark black and orange outline. The contours of the spot I'd picked out read as solid, safe to land on, so I gave Pinky a nod and he flicked the Window back to normal view. A few tugs on the controls later, and the ship settled to the ground, gentle as you please, with only a faint crunch marking our contact.

"Well done," Sirena said. "Do we get to go exploring now?"

"We should take some samples and do analysis first," Marta said. "You never know what's out there."

"Oh poo. I can see my little world is perfectly friendly. Clear skies, soft breezes, placid water."

Pinky swiveled his eyespots around the featureless stump of his head toward Sirena. "Your Highness surely didn't travel halfway across the Empire to be laid low by the Uncommon Cold."

The princess quirked a lip. "No, I suppose not. Gather your test tubes, then. I'm off for a swim. Do let me know when it's safe to debark." And with a gentle whir of her gravchair, the scion of Atlántida soared out of the bridge.

I heard Peter mutter behind me. "I miss my shop."

"How many little scouts have their own swimming pool?" I said with a smile, swiveling to face him.

"Yeah, that I'm not even allowed to use." A frown creased his broad face.

Marta wrinkled her nose prettily. "You wouldn't want to anyway, what with the fish and the seaweed." She laid a hand on Peter's muscled forearm. "I'd rather our room weren't cluttered with your junk, too…"

"Junk, huh?"

"…but it's a fair trade for the chance to explore new worlds," she added quickly.

"I suppose that's fair," Peter said, his angular face softening into a smile. His fingers entwined with Marta's, and they leaned in for a kiss.

I swiveled back to the Window, feeling my cheeks warm up. I waited for what I felt was a perfectly reasonable length of time. Finally, I cleared my throat. "Um, why don't you get started on your tests, Marta?"

She took a moment to answer. "Hmm?"

I tapped my panel, looking straight ahead. "Your tests?"

"Right! I'm on it, chief."

"I'll go with you," Peter said. I heard both their footsteps as they shuffled out of the room.

I blew my breath out in a gust and turned to Pinky. "Those two..." They'd been more affectionate than usual on this leg of the trip. Maybe it was the excitement of having finally gotten somewhere. It shouldn't be bothering me.

Pinky gave me a three-armed shrug. "I remember when it was you two."

"Yeah, but not in public like that," I said, which was mostly true.

"Utterly shameless," Fareedh chimed in, but he was teasing me, not chiding them. He stood up and stretched his skinny limbs, catlike. Then he grinned, a bright smile against his dark features, his deep brown eyes shining. "Let's see if we can't beat those two into suits and see what this world's all about."

Marta and Peter were still putting together their experiments by the time Fareedh and I had fully suited up. I smiled at the sharp contrast we made, the two of us crammed into the tiny airlock: me short and solid in my boring beige environmental suit, while his rainbow-colored one clung to his body, making him look even ganglier than usual.

"Just like old times," I said, double-checking my helmet seams. My voice was a little more brittle than I'd expected.

His reply came loud and clear through the suit comms, and simultaneously through the outside air, muffled by the bubble of plastic over my head. "Not quite. The stakes aren't so high this time."

"Aren't they?" I asked.

Fareedh looked at me, waiting for me to go on.

"I'll concede that we're not out of gas on a creepy dead world, but if this planet pans out, it could mean everything for us."

He put a hand on my shoulder, steadying me while I plugged an oxygen bottle into the back of my suit.

"And if it doesn't," he said, "we just go to the next one."

"We're in a hurry, remember?"

Fareedh's smile was broad and effortless. "It's a good thing *Majera's* a fast ship, then. Anyway, you're the one who always tells us not to borrow trouble." He reached for the wall panel behind him. "Speaking of which, let's be sure to be good guests while we're here." Fareedh tapped the wall panel with a gloved hand. The lights of the room shifted from ambient gold to harsh blue as decontaminating radiations played over our suits.

"I'd almost forgotten," I said. "Marta's worried about bugs getting us, but I'd hate to hurt whatever's here." I let out a breath and nodded at my friend. "And thanks, you're right."

The panel gave us a self-satisfied *ping*, and the lights went back to normal.

"That's that," Fareedh said. He looked at me and waggled his thick eyebrows. "Shall we?"

At my nod, he cycled the airlock. The good air in the room hissed away into vents, leaving us momentarily in vacuum. Then the doors opened and alien air entered in a rush, staggering me a little. Through the opening, I saw a vast green field dotted with tree-like growths. A few hundred meters away, the green merged with the deep blue of the ocean. Outside was a whole new world to explore.

"Helmi Kader, eat your heart out, "I said with a grin and stepped off of the duralloy floor of the ship.

...and promptly sank ankle deep in water.

"What the hell?" I yelped, hands flailing. I grabbed onto the nearest solid thing, which turned out to be Fareedh.

There was another voice in my ears, Pinky's: "Everything all right out there?"

"I thought deep radar showed this spot as solid," I groused.

Fareedh pointed to his feet. I followed the gesture and saw his boots were on dry land. Of course.

"You just got unlucky," he said, "There's ridges we can walk on." He helped me onto his patch of high ground and pointed out a path.

Aside from the swampiness of our immediate locale, it certainly *looked* like a good world. The surroundings and plants looked terrestrial, though Marta would be the authority on that. Still, that anything was growing was something of a coup. Life isn't uncommon in the universe, but fully developed ecosystems along familiar lines are. It looked like a nice spring day on Vatan. I checked the outside temperature: 280 K, not much above freezing. All right, we'd need jackets if we took off our heated suits, but it was still doable.

Fareedh struck out in the direction of the beach. I followed in his footsteps, shaking out my dripping boots as I went. After a few minutes of carefully picking our way, our strides grew more confident. The difference between the moss-covered puddles and the slightly higher berms had became easy to tell.

Movement caught my eye. Just a couple of feet to my left was something dark crawling on a bunch of legs.

"Take a look at this, Fareedh!"

'This' was about a quarter meter in diameter, kind of like a crab but with more legs. The thing skittered toward me. I watched it in fascination.

"Careful, Kitra," I heard Fareedh say. But the thing stopped a couple of meters away and just sat there, perhaps unsure if I posed a threat. I was pretty sure it wasn't a threat to *me*. Environmental suits are tough, and it didn't look like it had teeth big enough to puncture it. If it even had any teeth. I knelt down so as to not be as imposing. The creature wiggled a little but didn't run away. We waited there together for a bit, Fareedh unmoving ahead of me. I thought of snapping a holo with my *sayar*, but I didn't want to scare it. Eventually, the little thing seemed to make up its mind about me, wandering nonchalantly into a green-topped puddle and disappearing.

"Take us to your leader," Fareedh called after it.

I chuckled. "If they have one. Well, we know this planet has animals now. That's a bonus, right?"

Marta's voice rang in my ears, "You got samples without me?"

I turned and saw her and Peter emerging from the ship. His suit was a subtle pink, hers a vivid green.

"Don't worry," I said. "We'll still name them after you."

Pinky's voice cut in again, "You shouldn't complain. I'm the one stuck on the ship."

"You hate wearing suits, anyway," Peter said.

"That's true. I'm a confirmed nudist."

Marta drew a vial from her belt pouch and scooped up a bit of pond water. "Well, let me run some tests. Maybe it'll be safe to run around naked."

"*You* can run around naked," I said, scuffing my boot against the moss. "I'll take this suit over my birthday suit, thank you very much."

"Humans and their prudery," Pinky scoffed lightly.

We scouted around a while longer, trudging through the moist greenery. I didn't see any more crabs, but there were smaller animals, grey and scarab-like. We had animals like this on Vatan, but they were all imports from original Earth specimens. Vatan's life had been mostly confined to the ocean when settlers first got there.

Glowworm's ecosphere was clearly more diverse than that. Not "advanced." Marta had lectured me many times that evolution doesn't go in straight lines. Overhead, there was some kind of flying or floating life, lazily drifting. As we ventured closer to the ocean, the plants got taller and more dense until, by the time we reached the beach, it was practically a forest of narrow-trunked trees. At least, that's how I mentally categorized them.

Through the trees, the shore beckoned, brilliant and sandy. I called up the external conditions display and saw that it was now up to an almost balmy 284 K outside; we'd been out long enough for the sun to get appreciably higher in the sky. I became conscious of the emptiness of my stomach. My *sayar* said three hours had passed, which meant a day was about 30 hours long. We still had plenty of time.

"I think it's lunch time," I said, but quickly saw that I was alone. I looked around, puzzled. When had I lost sight of everyone?

"Peter? Marta?"

"We're over on the south side, Kitra," Peter's voice replied. "You can see our transponders on the map. We went the opposite way. Marta's taking holos."

"Oh, then where's Fareedh?"

"He should be right next to you, according to my *sayar*."

I called up a map of the area and, sure enough, Fareedh's little rainbow dot, cycling through the colors of the spectrum, was close by. Off a little to my right. I pushed aside rubbery branches and stepped into a brightly lit clearing. Fareedh was there, standing out like a beacon in his wild suit. He wasn't moving, though, and he was holding his hands up oddly.

"Fareedh, what's going on?"

He didn't say anything, just jerked a finger in front of him. Then I saw: a suitless short man with thinning brown hair, dressed in a black robe, about ten meters ahead at the edge of the clearing. His right hand gripped the handle of something smooth and with a tapered tip, which he pointed unwaveringly at Fareedh. With the other hand, he pressed his finger to his lips. I froze, a scream half-formed in my throat.

Chapter 5

The stranger cautiously walked closer to us. His pale face was uncovered and the robe certainly wasn't airtight or armored. Evidently, *he* represented the most dangerous species on the planet. His blue eyes shifted from me to Fareedh and back again. He seemed uncertain, as if waiting for something. Then he put his free hand to his ear and a cruel little smile played on his lips. A moment later, I heard Marta's voice call out. "Peter! There's a…" Her voice cut off. I tensed, my heart racing.

At the same time, the man visibly relaxed, put his hand down, then jabbered a fast string of words at us that I couldn't make out.

"Wh… what?" I asked. It came out as a squeak.

The robed person sighed. "I will speak more slowly for you." I realized he'd been speaking French, or some flavor of it, anyway. "You are trespassing. Drop your *sayars* and take off your helmets."

"But…" Fareedh protested. The man gestured impatiently, and Fareedh reached for his helmet. Sweat prickled my skin. We would be out of communication with the ship, and I could only guess that Marta and Peter had been waylaid too. Numbly, I let my *sayar* fall to the ground next to my foot and undogged my helmet. I thought of holding my breath, but what was the point? Instead, I dropped the bubble of plastic and flinched against the cold air. I inhaled an odd but not unpleasant lungful.

"Who are you?" Fareedh was asking.

The man snorted. "My name is Etienne, but that isn't important. What's important is that this is Pureté, our planet, and you should have known better than to break the law by coming here."

"But this is an open system," I blurted.

"It is not. It is ours. Pureté is a sanctuary from the venality and corruption of the Empire." Etienne spoke with exaggerated enunciation to ensure he was understood.

Underneath the fear, I felt irritation. This was ridiculous. Planets were big enough for dozens of colonies, even one with just a single continent. Who was he to claim the whole thing? On the other hand, he had the gun, and there were presumably more people with guns.

"Look, this is just a big mistake," I said. "We only want to get some fuel and go. You'll hardly know we were here."

"It *is* a big mistake," the man said with a nod. "You trespassed with the intent to steal what's ours."

Fareedh spoke with far more calm in his voice than he could possibly have felt, "We'll happily pay for the water. We didn't know anyone had settled here."

The man eyed us warily beneath shaggy eyebrows and seemed to consider Fareedh's offer. Then he shook his head. "No, I think not." He waved his gun with a carelessness that made me even more nervous. "Once you landed on Pureté, you surrendered your belongings to us, so you have nothing to offer. Except, perhaps, the opportunity for us to give you salvation." He looked at us with disdain. "Though I can't imagine you're much worth saving."

At my expression, he added, "Oh, don't worry. You won't be killed or eaten. We're not savages. We'll just put you to work. We can always use more hands to grow the village. And eventually, you'll come around and forget your sinful Imperial ways." He gestured toward the trees with his gun. "All right. You two come with me," he said.

"What are you planning to do?" I asked.

"Impound your ship, take what we can use, and then dismantle the cursed thing."

My eyes widened. "You can't do that!"

"We can, and we will." He waved his gun. "Now move!"

Again, Fareedh looked at me. To his wordless question, I returned a dismayed nod. There wasn't anything we could do. The settler was armed. He could shoot both of us before we made it a meter, even swipe us down at the same time if his gun was fully charged. I shifted my weight to move as he had ordered.

There was an odd whine, faint but growing, like a mosquito diving at my ear. The settler heard it too; his eyes darted around looking for the source, though he kept his gun trained on us. Too late, he looked up. A mirror-surfaced bubble, hurtling straight down, covered him in a growing shadow.

He managed a strangled "Mon Dieu!" and a single shot, a blue beam sizzling the air with a faint crackling sound. The bubble moved in a blur, sparks flying from its underside. Then it smacked him down heavily, pinning him sprawled beneath it. Fareedh and I both ran to disarm him, but Fareedh beat me to it. It didn't matter. The gun had flown out of his hand, and sat beyond his reach.

The bubble shimmered out of existence, revealing Sirena in her grav chair, her teeth sparkling.

"Hello, darling. It sounded like you could use some help." Her hair was wet, vividly copper. She must have been showering or in the pool.

"Just a little," Fareedh said, returning the princess' smile. "Are you all right?"

Sirena's grav chair made weak clicking noises. It remained on the ground, balanced upright on its blunted point on top of the immobilized man's back. The antigravity was working to some degree, or the man would have been a lot more uncomfortable.

"I'm fine, but I'm afraid I'm stuck." She waved us away. "No, don't help me yet. Go find Marta and Peter." I bit my lip, hesitating. "Go on!" she urged. "This fellow's not going anywhere."

"Yeah, but there could be others. Fareedh, please stay with her." I pointed to the feebly struggling settler. He didn't look badly hurt, just stuck. "And keep your eyes on him." I glared at the man trapped under Sirena's chair. "Don't even think about calling for help," I said, though I wasn't sure what Fareedh or I would do if he did.

I darted out of the clearing. I had a rough idea where the others were based on Peter's last call. When the trees started to thin out, I slowed down. I wasn't sure exactly where the other settler was (or if there was more than one), and if they saw me, they could pick me off at almost any range if they had beam pistols. I caught a snatch of a conversation on the wind. A voice I wasn't familiar with, too muffled by distance to make out the words. Peter responded, his tone pitched higher than normal with fear.

"Mon dieu!"

I peered around the smooth gray edge of a tree trunk. Peter was about 20 meters away, his back to me. Marta stood in front of him protectively, calf deep in a puddle. Her sample kit spilled around her, some of the vials floating. Neither of them had their helmets, and about five meters in front of them, to their right from my perspective, was another figure in a robe. Aside from a beard, this one resembled the first, possibly a cousin or even a brother. I couldn't make out exactly what they were saying, but the colonist was agitated. He was armed, too. He barked a command.

I should've taken the first settler's gun. It would've been a clear shot. But I'd never fired one. And Fareedh and Sirena would've been left defenseless. I went to my knees. Searched for something. Anything. A distraction or, at last resort, a weapon. My hand closed over a hefty rock. I could circle around, clock him on the head from behind. It didn't look likely. Cover was sparse. Springy domes of bushes dotted the field. Nothing I could hide behind, even as short as I was.

There was a flicker of movement behind the colonist. I blinked. Nothing. A frond shifted by a gust of wind? Again, the motion. My mouth dropped open. A plant. *A walking bush* coming straight for him.

No, not a bush. A convincing copy! Stealthily moving closer, stumpy little legs were revealed. Pinky! He'd molded shapewise and mottled his color to mimic a native plant! The trick wouldn't pass a close look, but it was perfect camouflage for the area.

That cocky alien was getting too close, though. Any minute, the man with the gun might turn around. My best friend would be a sitting duck. I had to help him. Somehow.

"Here goes nothing," I muttered, hurling the rock I'd picked up in the gunman's general direction. I let out a holler, waved my arms, and then flung myself on the ground. Mud splattered my face. There was a crackling sound and the smell of ozone as a bolt of energy streamed over my head. I froze, my ears straining for the sound of the next shot. If the guy could see me, I was done for.

I heard another beamer shot followed by a loud cry. I went cold. My lips formed a silent prayer. If Pinky had been hit…

"C'mon out, Kitra!" Pinky's cheerful voice was the most beautiful sound I'd ever heard. I got to my knees and brushed the grime off my face. Peter had the bearded man on the ground in a hammer lock. Behind him, Pinky was returning to his more typical shape: four feet tall, with three legs and two arms. The right arm was oversized and powerful-looking. He must have smacked the guy good.

Marta scanned the distance for danger. Catching sight of me, her face lit up. She ran toward me, boots splashing, tripping over the final steps just as I was getting up. Marta lurched into me and wrapped me in a tight hug.

"You're okay!" she said, her voice cracking a little.

"*I'm* okay? I was worried about you!"

She let me go and brushed a ringlet of hair from her face. "Pssh," she said. "We had everything under control." Marta took my hand and trotted me back to the others. Peter looked up and a grin spread across his pale face. "Hey, hero. Nice work."

"You're looking pretty heroic yourself, mouse," I said.

Pinky snorted, which for him was a whole-body affair. "And what about me?"

The man on the ground wriggled. "You're all sinners. Trespassing Imperial heathens. Let me go!" His cheeks were red above his scraggly facial hair.

"Fat chance," I said.

Peter gave the guy's hand a twist, and he stopped struggling. "This is a lot of fun," Peter said in a tone indicating it was anything but, "but we've got to get out of here. There must be more of them."

"We have to go pick up Sirena and Fareedh," I said firmly.

"Sirena left the ship?" Marta's eyes were wide.

Pinky had settled into his new shape, his rubbery skin smoothing out and back to its typical pale pink color. "She sure did. I called her out of the pool when I saw you guys were in trouble. As soon as it was clear that the air was breathable, Sirena was out the airlock." He spread his arms in a shrug. "I got here as quickly as I could. She's faster than me."

I gave him a warm pat on his 'head'. "You did just fine. Look, you and Marta go back to the ship. I'll take Peter to where I left Sirena."

Marta started to protest. She'd picked up the settler's gun and was holding it with what looked like practiced ease. "It's dangerous out here, Kitra."

"I know, but the ship can't be left uncrewed, and no one's going to travel alone." I turned to Peter. "And I need you with me. Sirena's chair was shot. If you can fix it, great. Otherwise we'll need your strength to carry her."

Peter looked doubtfully down at the robed character, who looked lasers back at him. "What about this guy?" Peter asked.

Marta fished one of her pouches out of the puddle and withdrew a small cylinder. "Leave it to me," she said cheerfully. Then she stabbed the little device into the colonist's neck. He gave out a surprised gasp and then went limp, his eyes closed.

"Anesthetic," she explained. "He'll be out for an hour."

I held out my hand. "I need some of that for my guy."

Marta pressed the injector into my hand. Then she gathered the rest of her gear, gave Peter a quick kiss, and retrieved and dogged her helmet. "Come on, Pinky." Then she was off, Pinky waddling after her with a three-legged gait.

Sirena and Fareedh were right where I'd left them, Fareedh holding the swiped beamer close to his chest. I realized too late that I should have announced my presence loudly so he wouldn't think I was one of *them*. It didn't matter, though; Fareedh waved his other hand casually at me, clearly unworried. Either he was really confident in me, or he'd overheard what had happened. I guess we hadn't been quiet.

His smile broadened when he saw Peter. "Glad you made it out."

"I had some help," Peter replied. He walked over to Sirena and gave her an ironic bow. "Ma'am. Your ride got shot?"

"Just a bit," she said.

The settler underneath called out, "You shall pay for your arrogance." He was entirely too energetic. I raced up to give him a shot in the shoulder from Marta's injector. Luckily, they're pretty foolproof. It was a relief to see the man's eyelids close and his body still.

"Well done, darling. A very tiresome man." She looked over at Peter. "Do I need to get out?" Her tone was reluctant.

Peter went to his knees and inspected the chair. "I don't think so. You're just lucky the hit didn't make it all the way through." He pulled out some kind of tool from his belt, ran it over the smooth surface of the chair near the point, and the panel covering the damaged portion came loose. It looked bad to me, but at least there was no sparking anymore.

"Can you fix it?" I asked.

"We'll see."

Tense minutes went by as Peter fiddled with the charred innards of the grav chair. I felt an itching in my back, like a target had been tattooed there. At one point, there was a rustling in the trees. Fareedh whirled to face it, beamer extended, but it was just one of the planet's floating creatures taking flight after... I don't know, feeding I guess.

Finally, I heard the faint sound of whirring as Sirena's chair returned to life, and when I turned, I saw it floating a few inches above the ground.

I blew out a breath I hadn't known I'd been holding. "Ready to go?"

Sirena tested the chair, spinning it in a full circle. "Good as new," she said. "You're a miracle-worker, Peter. I don't pay you enough."

He got up and shrugged wide shoulders. "Don't thank me yet. It's a patchwork job. I just hope it holds till we get back to the *Majera*."

Going back in took a lot less time than I thought it would, but then, we weren't meandering and exploring. We just had to mind the puddles. As it was, we splashed through several in our hurry, at one point scaring an entire hive of silvery beetles.

By the time we got back to the ship, Sirena's chair had started to whine ominously. We had to take turns going inside; the airlock only handled two at a time. Fareedh and I watched the treeline nervously, our backs against the ship, while Peter and Sirena went inside. It was a big relief when Peter signaled that they'd shucked their suits and had gone through decontamination.

Marta was waiting for us when we were desuited and finished our cleaning cycle. She quickly ran something over mine and Fareedh's bare arms. "Broad-spectrum antibiotic," she said. "Just to be safe."

"Good thinking," I said, "but first things first." I brushed past her, into the wardroom and onward to the bridge. Pinky was sitting in his seat and I saw that the lift systems were ready and standing by.

"You're way ahead of me," I said, jumping in the pilot's chair. I lifted the ship. Once I'd gotten a few hundred meters of air between us and the ground, I felt a whole lot better.

I turned to Pinky. "Well, where do we go now?"

"It's a big planet," he said, calling up a world map. "I can't imagine these Puritans can have expanded very far." I smiled grimly. I guess the settlers of Pureté *would* be puritans, and most likely Puritans with a capital "P". The kind of religious zealots that always seemed to end up on the frontier.

"I'm annoyed I missed them in the first place." Fareedh had come in. He sat down heavily in his chair and leaned back.

"How could you have known?" I asked.

He waved his hand over his panel, and a close-up view appeared in Window next to the virtual globe. I narrowed my eyes, wondering what I was looking for; it was just anonymous green hills to me. While I peered, I heard Marta and Peter shuffle onto the bridge.

"These guys must have built mostly underground using native materials," Fareedh said. "Good camouflage and obscured from deep radar. Still, the clues are all there. Look at the regular spacing of those clearings, and the discoloration here and here." Little purple highlights appeared to illustrate his words.

Peter shook his head, patting Fareedh's shoulder. "There is *no* way anyone could have caught that."

Fareedh shrugged his eyebrows. "I will next time. I'm coding an automatic alarm for patterns like this."

"Can these ruffians *really* have title to this planet?" Sirena looked at the hidden settlement disdainfully. Despite the last hour's adventure, she looked completely unruffled.

"I didn't see any record of it on Hyvilma," Marta said. "They might have registered at Sennet, though. Or maybe not at all."

"Squatters," Sirena sniffed.

Peter gestured with one hand. "We could report them, maybe."

"Or find another spot," Pinky added. "It's unlikely they've settled the entire land mass."

The princess shook her head, elaborate coral earrings jangling softly. "No, darling. I never liked this planet anyway. Too cold. Let's go out further and see what we can find. As we say on Atlántida, never get married on the first offer."

I opened my mouth to argue the point. Jerk squatters or not, it was a good world. But Sirena's cold look ended the discussion, and she was the client. I closed my mouth and looked over at Peter. "What about fuel?" I asked.

He nodded. "We'll need more." He got up and put a hand on mine and Pinky's chairs, surveying the Window's map of the planet. "There's a decent-looking spot over there; looks like a good thousand kilometers away. We can drop down there and do a quick fuel-up."

"Plus, we have guns now," Pinky noted. "Very obliging of our hosts."

I gripped at the controls. "All right, then. Over the sea we go."

Majera hit Mach 5 in less than a minute, leaving the little colony of Pureté far behind.

Chapter 6

I laid back on the fueling pipe watching the clouds go by, white and puffy against a brilliantly blue sky. The trees were different, though: gray spikes about three feet tall. They added to the inhospitable feel of the place. No flying animals dotted the sky, and I'd only seen a few land animals. They were small, hard-shelled things darting across the moss-covered permafrost. The wind picked up, making me shiver, and I wrapped my coat around me a little more tightly.

All in all, it was a lousy place to set up a colony.

Which is why we'd chosen it as the refueling spot. It was a place I didn't expect the Puritans to have settled. I was still worried that they might come after us, though that was fading. Neither Marta nor Fareedh had detected any sensor radiation on the way out, and in the last two days, we hadn't picked up any drones or vessels to the limits of our sensor range. The Puritans might well not even have such things anymore. Or even detectors. We'd been unlucky enough to land on one of their colonies, maybe their only one. We might never have noticed them otherwise.

But we had found them, and their presence here complicated things. Maybe they hadn't expanded beyond their original base. Maybe they wouldn't bug us if we settled somewhere else. But there was no way to be sure. Anyway, Sirena had made her choice. She didn't like this world and wanted to move on.

The broad pipe under me rumbled gently as water from the nearby shore coursed through on its way into the *Majera*. There, it would first be split into its hydrogen and oxygen atomic components, and then the hydrogen further split into its isotopes. The heavier deuterium and tritium that powered our fusion plant would get stored in our tanks while the rest was vented out. It was a slow process but an easy one, thanks to the distiller Peter had gotten for this trip. And thank goodness for it. Zooming through a continent-sized hurricane on an oversized gas giant with *Majera's* fuel hatches open made for a good story, but it wasn't something I wanted to do on a regular basis.

I found my eyes closing, lulled by the hum of the pipe and constant breeze. I must have dozed for a while. The next thing I was conscious of was Marta calling for me. I blinked and took a deep breath before swinging my legs off of the pipe, bringing my feet to rest on the icy ground. At least it wasn't soggy.

"Hey," she said, coming toward me. "I've got something for you."

"What's up? I see you made a new dress." It was purple and pink with long sleeves. It looked warm, and it fit her snugly.

Marta smiled, stopped a meter from me and gave a demonstrative twirl. "It's a new pattern I came up with. I'm glad I got a chance to try it out."

"Nice not to have to wear a suit."

"Yeah, but better safe than sorry." She extended her hand, a little capsule between two fingers. I took it from her.

"Another booster?" I asked. Marta nodded.

I popped the pill in my mouth, and it dissolved with a burst of cinnamon. I smiled. Marta had remembered that was my favorite.

"Not that there's any real risk," she went on. "Our biochemistry is pretty different. We can't eat the life on this planet, and they can't eat us. That includes the macroscopic and the microscopic."

I covered up a yawn and then rubbed sleep out of my eyes. "I wonder what the Puritans are eating."

"Prepackaged food, maybe crops they're growing underground."

"You sound pretty sure."

Marta put her hands on her hips and looked over the mossy plain at nothing in particular. "They probably haven't been here too long. You can only do so much with hydroponics. We'd have seen fields if they were cultivating on a large scale. "

"Yeah. For people claiming a whole planet, they're not advertising their presence."

"They probably will, eventually. It will take work to clear the existing life to seed their own." She frowned. "There's another possibility, and it might explain their hostility."

"What's that?"

"Maybe they're worried about pirates. Fields would show up from the air pretty easily."

"As far as I'm concerned, *they're* the pirates."

A quick shrug of her shoulders. "Maybe. I try to put myself in their shoes."

"Marta, they were going to imprison us and break up the ship. They were a bunch of wackos."

Her laugh sounded forced. "I'm not saying I'm happy about that. But they might have been one of the unsanctioned sects."

"The Empire's pretty tolerant," I said.

"Sure. If you fit the mold."

"You have to be pretty out there to be on the unsanctioned list!"

"Finitism used to be unsanctioned," she said softly.

I opened my mouth to answer, closed it again, and looked down, feeling like a jerk. I'd never quite understood Marta and Peter's Finitism. She'd patiently tried to explain it to me, the idea of a living universe, all of its components aware and interconnected in some mix of quantum mechanics and magic, but it was beyond me. I hadn't held it against her, as some did. Being Jewish, I'd never had to face persecution. But Marta had to grow up facing prejudice. Peter, too, who'd gotten beaten up every week until he turned himself into a mountain no one wanted to pick on. I could see why Marta would be sensitive. The Empire had smashed Ääretömyys, the planet where Finitism had been born four centuries ago, and we were *still* taught about it in history class as a lesson about going too far against the grain.

"You're right. I'm sorry," I said at last. I felt her hand touch my shoulder, gripping it briefly, then releasing.

The crunch of boots on ice drew our attention. Peter was making his way down the pipe, looking at it through his *sayar*.

I called to him, "Everything okay?"

He looked up, flashed a quick smile and waved a hand before returning his attention to the pipe. I stood up, walked a few paces away from Marta, and waited.

"Hey," he said in greeting when he got close, resting a hand on the pipe.

Marta put an arm around his shoulder. "Aren't you cold?" she asked.

Peter looked down at himself as if just realizing he was in shirt-sleeves. "Oh, nah. You know I run hot."

"Anything wrong?" I asked, looking meaningfully at his *sayar*.

He stuck it in his pocket and shook his head. "Nope. Just wanted to check the flow." Peter shrugged and smiled. "Something to do. Now that we know the planet is safe, I reasoned it would be nice to get some fresh air while I could."

Marta looked around the spikey forest wistfully. "It's too bad we can't stay longer. I'd love to get samples from at least three more places. You know, I haven't found any overlap in species between this spot and the first one?"

"Is that significant?" Peter asked.

"Not necessarily. But I can't know without more data."

I leaned back against the pipe, feeling the rumbling flow underneath against my palms. "There'll be other planets. When we find the right one for Sirena, it's guaranteed there will be stuff to look at there. Speaking of which." I got up and pulled out my *sayar*. "Pinky?"

"Yeah, boss?" his voice came from the device without delay.

"We know where we're going yet?"

"I think so. Have a look."

I held out my *sayar*, and Pinky sent me a starmap of the trans-Frontier area. It floated in three dimensions above the device.

"We're here," he said, a little picture of the *Majera* appearing over one of the stars. "This is GM 115." The map centered on another orange star about two parsecs away from GM 106, too far for a direct jump from Hyvilma. Its planets were displayed as a series of orbital circles. They all looked rocky in composition.

"Why that system?" I asked.

"A huge stroke of luck, actually. We already knew Planet One was in the water zone, but we couldn't be sure of its mass or its composition. It turns out the system's ecliptic is edge-on to this one. Better still…" The *sayar* switched to a light-curve/spectrograph display.

Marta squealed. "You got eclipse data! And look—water and oxygen."

I leaned forward. "It's unclaimed?"

"As unclaimed as this planet, for what it's worth," Pinky's voice said.

Not a whole lot," Peter said, a muscle flickering in his cheek. "I worry about Jumping blind at the edge of our range. And there's no gas giant in the system as a back-up plan."

"Because I really want to do that again," I said drily.

"There's definitely water on One," Pinky said, "and I'm getting scatter from further out that suggests planetoids. If we get really desperate, we can park on an ice ball and melt what we need. Plus, we'll have enough in our tanks for a one-parsec Jump, and there's at least one system with a gas giant in range from there for that."

"Planetoids or another Jump; either way, that'll make for slow fueling," Peter said.

I looked at Marta. "We okay for food?"

She nodded. "Six more weeks, easily."

I did the mental math. Another week to the new place, a week back to here or to another pit stop for refueling, two more weeks to Hyvilma. That left a two week margin for contingencies. Not great, but doable. And the sooner we took off, the better.

I looked back along the gray line of the pipe, to the wedge of our ship. Then back at Peter.

"Seems like a good risk." I said. "Of course, it's up to Sirena."

"I guess I'm game," Peter said. "I mean, it can't be more dangerous than here was, right?"

Chapter 7

You're not supposed to look at hyperspace.

I'd told myself that before I unblanked the Window. A little voice kept repeating that in the back of my mind while the rest of me reeled. As I watched the swirling nothing in front of me, a random thought went through my mind. A memory of an article I'd read about the Bugs, the newest alien race to be discovered. They see more dimensions than us, the trade-off being that they always seem distracted and cranky. It's claimed that they can even make some sense of hyperspace. I wouldn't know. I'm not a Bug.

Hyperspace doesn't really have a color. A holo pointed at a ship's Window just shows an innocuous medium gray, but that's not at all accurate. I'd only seen raw hyperspace once, the time *Majera* had slipped itself into Jump on our maiden flight from Vatan. It had squirmed, reaching right behind my eyes without going through them. Ever since, it had dared me from behind opaqued screens, challenged from beyond thick duralloy. It was insanity to want to see it, this void that people instinctively shunned. And yet...

Once, when I was sixteen, I drove the ground road out to Mersin. Both of Vatan's moons had been below the horizon, and there was only the dim glow from the rings that arced across the southern sky. Something possessed me to switch the skimmer to manual control and then, after a moment's hesitation, turn off the headlights. It was terrifying, exhilarating, zooming along in almost complete darkness under the starry sky.

I *knew* that looking at unfiltered hyperspace was dangerous. I felt it. I stared anyway. Something visceral in me wanted to understand it, to know the nature of this place I plunged into a week at a time with only a metal cocoon as protection. More than that—I wanted to master it.

Slowly, shapes began to appear in the not-gray void, outlines becoming distinct. My eyes watered, and my head ached with the effort of focusing on them. Weird currents shimmered, separating into regular polygons: four, six, eight-sided. Then they blurred together in a spiral, making a roulette pattern like those mathematical curve plot games Pinky played on his *sayar*.

The patterns danced, now a pair of helices like dancing DNA sliding together and apart. They pulsed like a signal. Was it a signal? Was hyperspace trying to talk to me? I swallowed, though I could barely feel the dryness of my throat. Yes, there was something out there calling to me, I was sure. I just needed to concentrate a little longer. Now I couldn't look away even if I wanted to.

My eyes, strained to the limit, blinked on their own. When my eyelids parted, the pattern was gone, replaced with rough static. I growled in frustration. Then a panic welled up in me and, for a moment, my hand fumbled for the control to opaque the Window; my dry throat certainly wasn't up to giving the order.

The panic passed. No. Just one more try. I refocused, grappling with the chaos, trying to force it back into a semblance of order. But instead of becoming the polygons and helices again, it became an angry ocean, its wave crests little knives that stabbed out at me. I tried to fling up my hands to cover my face. They refused to move, gripping armrests that seemed kilometers away.

The gray sea became a hurricane that buffeted me like a flimsy kite, and now the pattern extended beyond the Window. Out of the corners of my eyes, I saw the bridge of my ship transformed, a cartoon of the cramped cockpit of my glider that I'd left back home on Vatan, dozens of light years away. Was this a dream? Or was my mind trying to make sense of hyperspace by translating it into something familiar?

I reached for the controls—glider controls now. This time, my hands obeyed. The part of my mind that knew this had to be an illusion receded to a far corner. I wasn't in Jump anymore. I was in a storm over Vatan, bigger than any I'd ever flown through. With a wrench at the flight sticks, I turned the craft's tail into the winds, letting them direct my course rather than batter the glider into pieces.

Clouds churned ugly gray over and around me, and the cabin shuddered. The ground and the sky were completely obscured. There was only my glider and the storm. I drove the piloting stick hard to the left and felt the craft's ailerons bite into the air stream. Wobbly but true, my glider navigated a course through the winds, safe for the moment.

The hurricane howled at me for my cleverness, cracking hammer blows against the plane's light frame. There was no way the glider could hold up much longer. I pushed forward on the stick, feeling my stomach lurch as the craft went into a dive. Streamers of dusty clouds went past the windows. Wind whistled through the shuddering walls of the fuselage. I peered out. Where was the ground? Surely there must be ground somewhere! I stole a glance at the altimeter, but its face was glazed over, unreadable.

The sound of the wind began to modulate, pitch lowering even as its force remained constant. It wailed, like an *olumperisi* from legend. The banshee screech froze the sweat on my skin and made my heart leap into my throat. The shriek softened, became a siren's song, the sound almost seeming to form words. I listened, eyes wide in horror and fascination. Again, there was the feeling of something trying to make a connection.

Then a giant's hand smacked the tail of the sailplane, sending it spinning. I flew out of my seat despite my straps, through the windscreen, into a pattern that looked like a pair of jaws snapping shut...

...onto the dull tiled deck of a starship.

A klaxon assaulted my ears, three blasts and a pause, three blasts and a pause. I came slowly to my feet, shaking my head. A group of kids in disposable spacesuits rushed around and past me, followed by a pair of oversized adults. The children squealed and cried while the grown-ups urged them on. I might as well have been a rock in a river for all they noticed me. A moment later, they were gone, around the corner. The children had been my height, I realized, the adults towering over me and them.

The alarm continued, and its meaning came to me: Decompression warning. Instinctively, my hands flew to my head. I felt reassuring plastic between my fingers and my face, and I breathed a sigh of relief. I was wearing a sealed suit.

I was dimly aware that this couldn't be real, that it had to be some kind of Jump-induced illusion. But the deck felt solid beneath my boots. The flat smell of bottled air was strong in my nostrils. Where was I? The size and shape of the corridor, not to mention the endless siren, made it clear I was on a starship, and one much bigger than *Majera*. Doors lined the hall, each marked with a nameplate. Their labels all began with "E" followed by a number.

I swallowed. I knew this place all too well, though it hadn't existed for more than a decade. Education deck: The school level on *L'émissaire*.

"Little one?" It was a woman's voice, strong but laced with concern, echoing down the corridor. I looked up and saw her standing where the hallway Came to a "T" shape to the port and starboard. Her uniform, the severe and tapered auburn suit of the Diplomatic Corps, was smeared with grease. She gestured to me, hand outstretched.

Tears blurred my vision. I lurched forward, clumsy on children's feet, and flung my arms out to her. "Mama!" I cried. We moved toward each other, ten meters, five. Our fingers had almost met when I saw the bright surge of spiraling polygons behind my mother turn her into a silhouette, her dark hair a wild halo…

"Kitra!"

I screwed my eyes shut as the world flared white. My gut wrenched, and I was falling, falling.

I became aware of my tightly curled fingers digging into the ends of my chair. My butt was sore from hours of sitting.

"Kitra, what are you doing?" The same voice as before. Not my mother's. A real person. Someone alive.

I opened my eyes. The Window was a non-threatening shade of cream. Someone had turned it off.

My throat wouldn't work. I swallowed once, twice. "I was just…" What had I been doing? The memories of the hurricane and the ship were shattered, receding far back into my mind, like a fading nightmare.

Marta swiveled my chair around and looked at me searchingly. Her eyebrows were knit with concern under stray brown ringlets.

"What happened?" I managed. The cool, dimmed light of the bridge's ceiling panels was like soothing water on a burn.

"The screen was on. You had your hands up, and you were crying out." She pushed my hair back and pressed a soft palm to my forehead. I wriggled under her touch and brushed her hand away gently.

"I'm all right."

"It's not safe, you know."

I took a deep breath and tried to smile. It didn't quite come together. "What are you doing up so late, anyway?" I asked. I'd thought everyone had gone to sleep when I went to the bridge.

Marta looked at me for a moment without a word. Then, "I wanted to check up on the new filter plants I'd set up in the wardroom. I've got sensors that will tell me if there's anything wrong, but, you know." Marta gave me the ghost of a smile. "Living things are finicky."

I leaned back in the chair, drinking in the solidness of the small bridge. Diagnostic displays cycled in multicolored sheets above the four other crew stations. The Tree glowed its mellow green. A soft, reassuring thrum underlay the whir of the ship's ventilators. My eyes lit on the back of Fareedh's chair, behind mine, decorated with a hand-painted double rainbow. It was all so familiar, normal. I blinked, took another deep breath.

"You sure you're all right?"

"Yeah." My smile was tight. "Don't worry. I won't be doing that again for a while."

Marta pursed her lips, clearly not convinced. Then she shook her head, her hazel eyes fixed on mine. "I'll leave you alone then." She turned and stepped toward the door.

"Don't wake Peter up," I called after her.

That brought out a ghost of a smile. "Oh, we weren't sleeping." She ducked her head to avoid bumping it on the jamb and closed the door behind her.

I swiveled back to face the opaque Window. It stretched halfway around the half-circle room, its edges glowing a faint silver. All it would take was a touch of my panel or even a short phrase, and the screen would show me the world outside again. The space between space. I felt my fingers start to move forward.

No.

I shivered, the tingle starting at the base of my spine and zipping to my neck, and my shoulders jerked. Reality was what I needed. Something solid.

"Ship's *sayar*, show me our route," I called out. The Window darkened and filled with stars like a fast twilight. A crooked line 25 light years long connected the yellow sun of Hyvmila to the orange star that was our destination. In-between were Son Duryak and... I sighed... Pureté. There was no dot showing the *Majera's* position since Lord only knew where a ship actually was at any given time during Jump. Instead, the last leg of our trip glowed more fiercely on the map, and little numbers above it counted down the seconds until egress from hyperspace.

I contemplated the big starless Rift on the map separating Hyvilma and the new frontier from the rest of the Empire. Here I was, barely 20 years old, and already poking at the edge of the known universe. I was in over my head far enough without playing peek-a-boo with Jump space.

With a grunt of disgust, I got up and headed toward the door.

I squinted at the bright lights of the wardroom. Had Marta left them on after heading back to her cabin?

"Hey, Kitra!" came Pinky's cheerful voice.

I put my finger to my lips. "You'll wake the princess," I hissed.

Pinky was seated across the wardroom table from Fareedh, currently two-legged and three-armed. He waggled his middle hand in front of his eyespots.

"Nah," he said in a lower tone. "All the doors are closed, and she went to sleep hours ago." He rolled his spiral eyespots across the table. "Your move, Fareedh."

They'd clearly only just started playing: all the pieces still in orderly rows. The game had the glossy sheen of something recently printed by our Maker. It looked like Shogi or Chess or some other ancient game, but Fareedh may well have designed and programmed it himself. He'd done a lot of the work on *Empires*, the signature game of our group.

Fareedh inspected the board, elbow up on the table, chin cradled in thin fingers. His dark hair was pulled back behind his head, grown long enough now for a short ponytail. I missed his poofy curls, but his new style showed off his sharply handsome features to good effect. He sat cross-legged, as usual. A dreamy half-smile played on his lips as he chose a piece and moved it forward. Then he looked up at me and the smile broadened.

"Good morning," he said.

"Good midnight, you mean. Everyone's a night owl all of a sudden. Why do you have the lights on so bright, anyway?"

"Just trying to keep my tan," Fareedh said, gesturing to his cheek. It was a deep brown, the same color as mine. The six days in Jump hadn't faded it much, yet.

Pinky's rose-colored body wriggled and turned almost mahogany. "If you would just apply yourselves…"

I instinctively stepped back. When Pinky changed colors in a hurry, it often had something to do with his digestion. He quickly reverted to his normal coloring though, his eyespots locked on the board as if nothing had happened.

"Is the ship all right?" Fareedh asked lightly.

"Huh? Oh yeah. Everything's fine," I said. "Just, you know, doing some final checks so we're ready for tomorrow."

He stretched languidly and nodded. "Makes se—"

"Your. Turn," Pinky interrupted with uncharacteristic impatience. Fareedh turned back to the board, and I went to the other end of the room to heat up the remains of dinner for a snack. Not that I was that hungry; I just wanted a reason to stay up a little longer with my friends. Their presence was a comfort.

It had been Marta's turn to cook, and she'd made more wonders with *seitan*. She'd discovered the miracles of wheat gluten on our last trip out, when our supplies had run low. Since then, it had been promoted from an emergency ration to a staple. The heater chirped and steam wafted off what looked just like breaded veal cutlets. I smiled as the savory aroma hit me.

"I made some tea," Fareedh said absently, thumb pointing to a pot by his elbow.

"It's a little late for caffeine."

"Don't worry. It's herbal." He pushed the pot toward me meaningfully. I pulled a cup from the Maker and sat down next to him. Fareedh radiated warmth, and between him, the food smells, the dappled blue-sky ceiling, and Marta's broad-leafed plants in the corners, it was all very cozy. My eyes started to droop. I watched the game progress, occasionally taking a bite or a sip of tea (it was too tepid for my taste, but the flavor was good). Even after several moves, I still couldn't make heads or tails of the game.

"Who's winning?" I asked. "Fareedh?" I saw that there were several of Pinky's pieces collected off the board on Fareedh's side, captures from previous moves.

Pinky folded his outer arms under his middle one. "It's too soon to tell. Victory's based on controlling area, not taking units."

"Oh, like *Empires*?"

"Sort of. It's more about the pattern you make than the size of the area you have."

It was the kind of game Pinky would be good at. I found myself silently rooting for him. I liked Fareedh a lot, and there was no question that he was cute, but Pinky was my oldest friend.

A yawn forced itself through my lips, widening my jaws to their full extent. "Excuse me," I said fuzzily. It was already 1:00 AM, ship time. "I really want to see how this turns out, but it's getting late."

"Don't worry," Fareedh said. "If *he* wins, we won't hear the end of it tomorrow. And if he loses, you just won't hear about it."

Pinky seemed to deflate and his rubbery skin turned a bright blue. "Every time you say hurtful things like that, I *dye* a little inside."

I rose to my feet, "It's definitely time for bed. Don't stay up too late. Tomorrow's a big day." I tossed my dishes into the Maker.

"Aye, aye, Cap'n," they said in unison, which felt pretty good until Pinky ruined it with a giggle.

Just one door separated my cabin from the wardroom, but once it was closed, it was like I was in a world of my own. The only sounds still audible were the omnipresent rumble of *Majera*'s power plant and the hiss of the air vents. I brushed my teeth and flopped on the bed, not even bothering to shuck off my clothes. I'd just fling them in the Maker tomorrow and print new copies of my usual shorts and a tank-top. I looked up at the ceiling, frowning. What if I printed something nicer? Jump-out days could be dress up days. Like a good-luck tradition. Marta'd be proud; maybe she could help me pick out a pattern.

I rolled over, my eyes drifting over the holo of Helmi Kader, striking a noble pose at her dig on Syr Darya. It still had pride of place on my wall, opposite the new sprawl Pinky had made for me. My gaze fell on the souvenir table next to the bed. It was still largely empty: A coaster emblazoned with the words *Le Frontiére* sat next to a little pink stone no bigger than my thumb, whose yellow flecks reflected the room light like captive stars. Near them was the pair of fossils Fareedh and Marta had given me, their display boxes open.

I smiled. *Someday, that table will be full,* I thought. Then my eyelids drooped, time sped up, and I was lost in slumber.

Peter let out the king of all belches as the *Majera* slipped out of hyperspace. Marta giggled. I reflexively looked over my shoulder at Sirena, but the corners of her lips were pulled up and her eyes twinkled. I had to smile. She was one of us now.

It was a smoother Jump than the last, partly because I'd told my pride to shut up and had taken a pill beforehand. My hands still gripped the flight sticks as the Window came back to life, filled with a perfectly ordinary starfield. I shifted, a little uncomfortable in my new blue dress. Maybe changing up my wardrobe had been a bad idea.

A long moment passed. Then Pinky called out, "Bullseye!" with not a little pride.

"Looks like deep space to me," I heard Marta say behind me.

With a dramatic flourish, Pinky swept his stubby fingers across his panel, and the Window's view whirled rightward—the same routine as last time, I noted. The full disk of a planet, spanning about half of the screen, glided into view. I heard a gasp, and then Sirena's accented voice whispered, "It's beautiful."

It really was. Where Pureté had been white with storms and ice, GM 115 #1 was a blue marble flecked with whorls of cloud. From the magnification numbers on the Window, and doing a quick calculation in my head, it looked like Pinky had come in at pretty close to the minimum safe distance. He might have been showing off, or it might have been an accident. Either way, it made me nervous. I made a mental note to talk to him about it.

Still, we'd made it. I let out my breath and turned to ask, "Have you got any numbers, Fareedh?"

He looked over at his display. "Give me a moment. The ship's *sayar*'s got to do some KeplerNewton."

The planet before us wasn't entirely blue, I saw now. A brown-and-green continent spanned much of the upper hemisphere. From its shape, I immediately dubbed it in my head "The Hand," though it looked less like a human hand than an appendage Pinky might make: a palm, three closely held fingers, and a thumb that jutted toward the equator.

"I've got data for you, Kitra," Marta piped up. "Spectrograph shows surface atmospheric pressure around 120 kilopascals, mostly nitrogen and oxygen. I don't see any sulfur dioxide, methane, or any other poisonous gasses in dangerous concentrations."

"So far, so good," I heard Peter murmur.

"Ah, here we go," Fareedh was saying. "Radius: 6,900 kilometers. Mass: 7.17 times 10 to the 24 kilograms. Surface gravity is .98 gee. "

I licked my teeth, feeling my eyes widen. This planet was as close to "Terran" type as I'd ever seen. It was too good to be true.

Fareedh went on, "Year is 332 standard days. A planetary day is… hold on… I'm following a landmark. Looks like it's around 20 hours. Hmm…" I turned to see why he'd trailed off and saw him shifting his jaw from side to side in contemplation. "It'll take a minute to figure axial tilt, but call it 20% for now."

"Oh how nice!" Sirena said. "We shall have lovely seasons."

"I'm afraid not," Pinky said. "Sorry, your Highness…"

"Sirena, darling."

"Sirena, darling," he echoed, keeping his coloration perfectly constant. "The planet's orbit is almost perfectly circular. And as you can see," Pinky filtered the Window for infrared, turning the planet into a nearly uniform glowing disc, "it doesn't look like there's much difference in temperature between the north and south hemispheres. The oceans probably moderate things too."

"Oh, poo…"

"The constellations will change throughout the year," Peter added quickly. "That should be fun."

Marta chimed in. "The weather patterns will be interesting, too, because of the tilt; not all boring bands fixed by latitude."

Sirena waved a hand, the bangles on her thin wrist jingling. "You don't need to humor me. It looks like a lovely world. And we'll have a romantic moon to light our nights, too."

Fareedh's expression went slack with puzzlement. Both he and Pinky exclaimed at the same time, "There is no moon!"

The princess gave a regal little chuckle and pointed. "What do you call that?" Her grav chair rose a meter off the floor so she had a clear view over mine and Pinky's heads.

Sure enough, a brilliant point of light had come into view from the right. It moved slowly but perceptibly, shining steadily.

"Yeah, Pinky," I said. "What *do* you call that?"

Fareedh was tapping at his panel again. "It's not a moon. We'd have seen tides, and the planet would wobble."

"Even if it was a small moon?" Marta asked.

"Any respectable moon," Pinky sniffed in reply.

"Nevertheless, there it is," Sirena said simply. I saw that her hands were now folded in her lap, her expression curious.

The Window flickered at the corner of my eye, and when I turned back, I saw the stars had disappeared and the planetary disk was dark charcoal with orange contours.

"I've turned on the deep radar," Peter explained.

I looked at the "moon", which was now a neon blue. My heart sank. It *had* been too good to be true.

"That's a ship, isn't it?" I said.

"Yeah," Peter agreed. "Or a space station."

"We got beaten here, too?" I blurted. Pinky extended a reassuring hand and patted me on the shoulder.

"Looks like it," Peter said. He sounded as defeated as I felt. That was that. We were near the end of our logistical tether. If we wanted to play it safe we'd have to go back to Hyvilma to stock up for another trip out. What a waste of weeks.

"Hmm. I'm not so sure." That was Marta. I swiveled the chair around, the hem of my dress rustling softly. She peered intently at her display.

"What do you mean?" Sirena asked.

"Well, I'm not hearing anything on any of the comm frequencies. Not from the planet or the station."

"We didn't pick anything up the last time, either," Pinky noted.

"They could be sending tight-beam messages," Fareedh added. "Or maybe they're using non-standard channels?"

"Maybe they're aliens?" Peter said, an edge in his voice.

Marta shook her head, curls bobbing. "It's got a standard transponder. Sorry, I should have led with that. It's Imperial. I could probably figure out what ship it is with a little research." She frowned, pretty dimples appearing at the corners of her mouth. "The power is really low, and there's hardly any other emissions, even infrared."

Pinky mimicked the sound of forlorn wind wailing. "WOooOoooOooo... it's a ghooooost ship."

Sirena made a quick, strange sign with her right hand over her brightly jeweled halter, first top to bottom, then left to right. "Ay, Dios mío. Don't say such things." The idea didn't thrill me either, and I felt a chill settle on me.

"It's big, whatever it is." Peter said. He'd focused the Window, turning the dazzling point into a fuzzy cylinder, twice as long as wide. "I'd guess it's a colony ship. And since the power output is low, they've probably made planetfall already and abandoned the ship."

"Double poo," Sirena said to that.

"Does that make sense?" Fareedh asked. "Why leave all that valuable material in space instead of landing it?"

"They might have used shuttles to offload the people and supplies and left the ship intact in case things didn't work out," Peter replied.

"Well, anyway, it's not hopeless yet," I said, trying to salvage both the situation and my spirit. "If there's a colony, maybe we can get supplies at least."

"Because that worked out so well last time," Peter said. Marta gave him a gentle shove.

Pinky waved a pink pseudopod at the unknown ship. "Do you want me to give that thing a wide berth?"

I thought about it, then shook my head. "No. In fact, I want to get a closer look. Deep radar didn't show any structures on the planet, and we're not picking up transmissions. It's possible the colonists have gone to ground like the Puritans, but that seems unlikely given that they left their ship up here announcing their presence."

"They might have settled on the far side of the planet," Pinky pointed out.

I nodded. "Sure, but if we're going to be sitting in orbit for another 90 minutes, we might as well check out that ship on the way and kill two flies with one shot." I rubbed the goosebumps on my arms. "I've got a weird feeling. Something's not right."

Chapter 8

It took about an hour and a half at one-half a gee's thrust to match orbits and close in on the mystery ship. By then, it was clear that there weren't any colonies on the far side of the planet. There couldn't be. The other hemisphere had no sizable land masses, though there were strings of archipelagos marking the tips of undersea mountain ranges. The back side of the planet was still mostly in shadow, but deep radar made it clear that there were no settlements of any size to be found. Marta was still coming up empty on the comm bands, too. All except the beacon on the bogey, the strange vessel, which we picked up more and more clearly as we approached: a set of chimes on three frequencies that said little more than "I'm here."

From our new vantage, the outlines of the unidentified ship were crisp. The sun was now almost perpendicular to it, leaving the cylinder half-lit. The curved hull and the flat end of the bogey were somewhat but not entirely smooth; its projections stood out starkly against shadows so dark that they revealed nothing underneath. The whole thing was big, almost as big as the Trans-Rift ferry. It had to have crossed the Rift under its own power, which meant there was at least a Type 5 Drive in there somewhere. That made it military, government, or corporate owned. It didn't look like any warship I'd ever seen.

"How close are we going to get?" Peter asked. He tried to keep his tone casual, but I heard the edge of nervousness.

"Close enough to know what's going on," I said simply. Then added quickly with a glance at Sirena, "If that's alright with you."

"I want to solve the mystery, too. Marta, is he still dead?"

"He?"

"The ship, darling. Ships are 'he' are they not?"

"She," Fareedh murmured.

"*Neither*," I said, a little too loudly. Peter suppressed a chuckle.

"Quite," Sirena said after the briefest of pauses. "How is the ship?"

"I'm able to get a better map of emissions from here, though Peter would be better at explaining what they mean."

"Right," Peter said. He did something, and the bogey filled the screen. It was painted in a muted network of colors, mostly hoops that girdled the vessel. "There's still power being generated. You can see the purple glow along the axis down at that one end. It's being transmitted throughout the vessel, too. But if that engine's as big as I think it is, it's putting out too little energy to be in anything but standby mode." Focusing on work had steadied his voice, or maybe a powered-down ship was less threatening.

"Oh, this is interesting," I heard Fareedh murmur.

"What's up?" I asked.

He was running a hand through his hair, one eyebrow raised. "If we can get close enough, or maybe inside, I can query their ship's *sayar*. It's got a public access channel."

"You can't do it from here?"

He shook his head. "Signal's too weak. I can tell a connection *can* be made, but I can't make one."

I frowned. I hadn't thought of actually boarding the thing. "How would we get in?"

Peter walked up and put a hand on my seat, the other pointing at the rainbow schematic in the Window.

"Ships this big usually have a dock or bay for tenders on the axis. It's probably not on this end of the bogey given the power paths. We'd need to go to the front."

I swiveled in my chair to look up at him, then to the rest of my friends in turn. It was too big a decision to make by myself. "Do we do this?" I asked.

Marta nodded without hesitation. "I think we have to check it out. If they've got a rightful claim, we need to confirm it. If they're in trouble, we have to render assistance under the Laws of Space." There were nods and rumbles of agreement.

I turned back to the Window, considering the bogey one last time. I'd deliberately put *Majera* behind the cylinder in the same orbit on instinct. It's much faster to dock with something passive when you're coplanar; you just slow yourself into a slightly lower orbit, which actually speeds you up because you're making a smaller circle, and then wait for the target to slide above you as you pass it. A quick bit of thrusting gets you right next to it, or in this case, in front, for docking. It's the kind of elementary operation a ship's *sayar* can do with ease — if it knows where it's supposed to end up after the maneuver. But we weren't sure where the bogey's dock was, and in any event, I was eager to do a little bit of orbital maneuvering.

I took the sticks and gave it a try. It was trickier than I'd thought. I handled the orbital change just fine, but as we passed under the mystery ship, I muffed the nudge back into its orbit, ending up slightly above the thing. Now it was gaining on us, looming closer and closer. Lord, the thing was enormous! I kept my cool and nudged the thrusters, spiraling in just ahead of the bogey. It was like playing tag with a hover bus. Finally, sweat on my forehead, I managed to "park" *Majera* in orbit just in front of the cylinder, maybe 100 meters away.

The bogey was an array of semicircles from here, the sun half-illuminating all of the raised surfaces. There were no external lights to guide us. It was only then that I realized how quiet everything had gotten. I let out my breath in a gusty exhale and heard the rest follow suit, followed by a nervous, high-pitched laugh that could have been Marta or Peter.

"Well, here we are," I said. "Are we going to have to put on suits and leap the rest of the way?"

"Are you serious?" That was Sirena, surprise heightening her accent.

"No problem," Peter said with a wry tinge to his words. "We do this all the time. You just load Pinky into the airlock, evacuate the air, and shoot him at the center."

"What happens when he goes 'boooiiiinnnnnnnng'?" Marta asked.

"What happens when I go 'splaaaat'?" Pinky replied, but he flushed an amused salmon color.

"I don't think we'll have to do any spacewalking," Fareedh said calmly. "I've got a strong signal here. I think I can query their ship's *sayar* and get it to open up."

I looked at him in puzzlement. "Aren't there security measures to keep that from happening?"

"Oh, sure," he said, smiling with a mysterious air. Then he grinned more broadly. "Actually, defensive protocols aren't very robust on civilian ships. It's not like they plan to repel boarders like in the old wet navies. And anyway..." he trailed off. Slim fingers played over his console and his eyes narrowed in concentration. "Yeah, I kind of expected this. The bogey's in emergency stand-by mode."

"Could that ship be, I don't know, hibernating?" I asked.

He shook his head, the short ponytail waggling. "That'd look different. The ship's *sayar* is completely open to external control, no defensive protocols at all, like it restarted from scratch." Fareedh looked fixedly at me. "I think something happened to the ship."

"That makes sense with what I'm seeing, too," Peter chimed in. "What little power there is isn't being distributed evenly. There are several middle decks that look cut off."

The sweat was clammying my underarms. What had we gotten ourselves into?

"So you can..." I coughed, cleared my throat. "You can cycle their lock so we can slide in?" I asked.

Fareedh nodded. "Yeah, I have full control."

Deep breath. Then, "Okay. Trigger their running lights if they've got any. If nothing explodes, I guess we're going in."

The docking system was obvious once Fareedh got it illuminated: a giant port ringed with purple and green lights. As we approached, Fareedh sent a command, and the giant door irised open. I half-expected a rush of sublimed vapor, but there was nothing. Was there no air on the bogey at all? With that thought lingering in the back of my mind, I maneuvered *Majera* inside. No antigravity tractors guided my ship; I had to do it all by thruster. Luckily, there was room to spare. The rim of the dock hatch slid overhead and below us as we went through, and suddenly the interior of the huge bay was lit up.

"Did you do that?" I asked Fareedh without turning.

"No, those were automatics."

The lights inside were feeble, giving the walls and catwalks a sickly look. There were two other vessels flanking the central axis, moored flat to the far wall. They were perpendicular to us, which meant there must normally be gravity in this area, "down" being toward the rear of the big craft. The two moored ships, each as big as *Majera*, were probably gigs for transporting cargo and people to and from the main ship. They probably didn't have Jump drives on them. I rubbed together the fingers of my right hand, moist with sweat. I needed to set the ship down securely in case the gravity came on again. Hmmm. It'd be a tight fit but...

I tapped the antigrav thruster, pivoting *Majera* on its base to be parallel with the wall. While I did that, I caught sight of the portal to space "above" us irising shut without a sound, trapping us inside. Great. Another quick thrust and we drifted gently toward the spot behind the aft ends of the two moored gigs. There was no feeling of impact, but a harsh clang came as we touched the deck, conducted from the bogey's deck through our hull. I trimmed the antigrav to keep us pressed against the bogey.

"Let's secure the ship with line," I said. "I'd rather not rely on powered systems."

Fareedh quickly volunteered, "I've got it, Kitra."

"I'm going with you," Pinky said.

"You hate wearing suits," Marta pointed out.

"I've got a flexi. Anyway, if we get in a tight spot, I'm the only one who might be able to squeeze out of it."

"Alright," I said. "I'll stick by the controls. If something happens, you turn tail and rush right back in."

"You don't have to tell me twice," Fareedh chuckled.

As Pinky followed Fareedh out of the bridge, I noticed he was growing another leg on his backside. He paused a moment at the brink, swiveling his eyespots to me and then down to the new appendage, long and narrow. A *tail*.

I smiled. For Pinky, that was subtle humor.

Fifteen tense minutes passed before the word came over comms: Fareedh and Pinky had suited up and gone outside. I set the Window to wrap-around, giving us a 360° view of the hangar bay. The light in the hangar was still dim, but it seemed to come from everywhere, and there weren't really shadows anything could hide in. Pinky confirmed that there wasn't any air to speak of in the bay, nor was any coming in. That was actually good. It made sense for the hangar deck to be in vacuum and the rest of the ship airtight. Maybe there was air on the ship after all.

Pinky scrambled around, spider-like, using the magnetized tips of his suit to maintain his connection to the deck as he tugged the ship's line out toward the bollards we'd brought. They were like cleats on a pier for small ships, but portable.

It was funny. It was the 29th Century, at least by the old calendar, and here we were tying off our ship like some pirate barque from a thousand years ago. In a normal situation, antigrav or magnetics would lock us into place, or there would be some kind of custom mount to hook onto, as I assumed the bogey's gigs were secured. But in this case, it seemed like the lowest tech solution would be the least likely to fail, and anyway, we had the anchor lines.

Fareedh and Pinky didn't have any trouble attaching the wall— well—floor mounts and hitching *Majera* to them. Nothing jumped out at the pair. Nothing happened at all, in fact. To all appearances, the bogey *was* a ghost ship. I shivered. I was getting Jaiyk flashbacks, except this felt worse, somehow.

I saw Fareedh wave his gangly arms, his rainbow-patterned suit a bright spot against the sallow duralloy of the hangar. "All secure," he said. "I was thinking of patching into the ship's *sayar* from inside and getting the status of the bogey."

"You can't do that from in here?" I asked, trying to keep my voice level.

"I might, but sooner or later, we're going to have to see what's going on. Pinky and I have air for six hours."

"And suiting up's a pain," Pinky added. "Since I went through all that trouble, I might as well make the most of it."

It didn't feel right staying behind while my friends were out there. I stood up. "I'll join you."

"Don't be silly," Pinky's voice echoed over the bridge speakers. "You can watch from back there, and if something happens, you'll be able to help us."

Peter touched my arm. "They're right. Besides, we'll be able to watch over their shoulders. Let them know if we pick up anything unusual."

I sat back down slowly. "All right, but if your suit holos don't work outside the hangar bay, I'm calling you back in."

"OK," they responded in unison. The Window retained the panoramic view of the bay, but two new displays popped up in the center: one from Fareedh's neck holo, the other from Pinky's, somewhere below his view plate.

Zero gravity maneuvers are hard if you're not used to them. I'd spent my entire life in some kind of gee field, whether natural or artificial. My only experience with free fall was in brief spurts for emergency training or in the antigrav amusement parks, the latter of which I sort of outgrew when I started soaring. I don't *dislike* weightlessness — you can't really be a good pilot if you don't enjoy that lurched stomach feeling — but I wasn't used to it.

Fareedh obviously was. He went to his knees, demagnetized his boots, and made a leap toward the center of the bay. It was graceful as a ballet, his limbs seeming sleek rather than skinny. I watched every moment of it, from the launch, through the expert mid-course somersault, to the precise landing at the closed axis portal that was his destination. I expected Fareedh to bow after a performance like that, but he just crouched and inspected the hatch.

Pinky, not nearly as graceful, crabbed slowly after him. Fareedh was already waving his personal *sayar* around, several displays appearing above it, by the time Pinky caught up. Fareedh's neck holo went from *sayar* display to sayar display as he inspected them. The effect was a little disconcerting.

"I'm plugged in," Fareedh said. "Getting environmental data from the rest of the bogey. Hold on. I can throw it to the Window." A moment later, a third display popped up with an all-text readout.

"It's in French," Marta noted.

I nodded acknowledgement. Further confirmation that the bogey had come from the Empire. A heading caught my eye: *Émilie du Châtelet*. Was that the name of the ship? The captain? I did a quick search on my *sayar*'s reference but the only entry I found was about a pre-Jump Earth mathematician, a contemporary of Newton.

"Marta," I called. "You want to do a registry search on *Émilie du Châtelet*?"

"Already on it," I heard her say.

The rest of the text on the new display was straightforward, a listing of decks and their status in a sort of shorthand. Power levels, air density, occupancy... hmm. Maybe the last was a cargo indicator? The power levels were all under 5% usage, though whether that was due to the standby status or damage was impossible to tell. Air pressure was nil throughout the ship.

Dead, was my first reaction. I shook my head. *Maybe just abandoned.*

"I've got it," Marta said. "*Émilie du Châtelet* is registered out of Gloire. Wow, that's almost Core sector."

"What is he, er, it?" Sirena asked. I turned around to face them.

"Colony ship, like Peter thought. 10,000 passengers and 100 crew," Marta said.

I chewed on that. "That thing is big, but it doesn't look like 10,000 people big."

Marta shrugged. "Cold sleep? The registry says it's got a Type 5 Drive. It'd still take more than two months to get here. That's a lot of time to feed so many passengers."

"It's like the ferry," Sirena noted.

I turned to look at the readout display again. Occupancy read 80-100% on five of the sixteen decks. On the others, the numbers were all 0%. Had some of the passengers been offloaded? I noted that the power levels on those decks seemed less stable, fluctuating from 0-1% as opposed to the flat 2% that was consistent along the other decks.

"I've got bad news," Peter said. "A colony claim's been registered under 'Gloire Nouvelle'."

The bridge speakers came to life with Pinky's voice, "No points for creativity," he said with a chuckle.

"The whole planet?" Sirena asked.

"It's not specific."

"How did we miss that?" I asked Peter.

He looked worried for a moment, then his face cleared as he reviewed his display. "It's got a pending flag on it. They haven't brought back proof of survey."

That was a relief at first. Then it sunk in. *Why* hadn't they completed the claim?

"Are you going in?" I asked. I leaned forward in my chair, my fingertips sliding against each other.

"If you're okay with it," Fareedh commed. "There's no air on the other side, so there's no risk in opening the hatch."

He meant no risk of decompression one way or the other. There was plenty of risk otherwise. I checked the display once more. If I was reading it right, the deck below the bay was one of the ones with steady power and full 'occupancy'. That was something.

"Go ahead, you two. We'll be watching."

Chapter 9

Watching was nerve-racking. Once Fareedh and Pinky were through the hatch, into the shaft that ran the whole axis of the cylindrical *Émilie du Châtelet*, they disappeared from *Majera*'s sensors. I suppose Peter could have sent a drone after them, but the effect would have been the same. We were now limited to what our vanguard could see, our view restricted to the holos of individuals, though we still had an overview of the situation from our tap into the *Émilie*'s ship's *sayar*.

Through Fareedh and Pinky's eyes, we saw what looked like a long corridor stretching into dim bluish distance. Had the antigrav been on, this would have been a vertical shaft. Presumably there was an elevator somewhere along it, but it wasn't working. My neck itched. If the gravity came on, the two of them would tumble hundreds of meters to their death.

I swallowed to moisten my throat. "Guys, do me a favor and get into the next level sooner rather than later. I'll feel a whole lot better when the floor is closer to your feet."

"Rodger dodger," came Pinky's flip reply. Through Fareedh's camera, I saw him clamber hand over hand over hand along the ladder that lined the hall. Fareedh's view went from Pinky to his own feet. The Window display that was tied into Fareedh's *sayar* kept changing displays, mirroring what he was looking at on his portable device.

Pinky quickly found a hatch leading into Level 16. It opened without resistance: unlocked, and with no pressure differential. "Vacuum in here," he said.

Both Pinky and Fareedh's holos went pitch black, and I felt my heart miss a beat. A constellation of stars faded into view as their holos compensated for the low luminosity. Some of the stars blinked off and on, like Eid-al-Fitr lanterns. They stretched on for what seemed like miles but couldn't have been more than a few dozen meters. Fareedh turned on his suit beams then, and a cone of brilliance stabbed through the airless chamber. I heard him gasp.

Rows upon rows of clear-faced coffins, each with a headboard of blinking lights. Cold sleep beds. I heard Peter clear his throat followed by a rustling of Marta's dress. I held my breath as the nearest bed became the object of focus, growing to fill the view as they drifted toward it.

Inside was a little girl, pale as ice, unmoving as a statue. Her hair floated around her narrow face like a dark, frosted cloud.

"Marta," Fareedh's voice called. "I'm patching you into the bed's diagnostics."

"Thanks." Her voice was thinner than usual.

A pause. Fareedh's holo seemed to focus on nothing; he must have been consulting his *sayar*. But Pinky kept his 'eyes' directly on the girl in the bed as if transfixed. I watched as one of his suited pseudopods reached out to touch the plastic. The coffin's occupant didn't look like she was asleep. She looked dead, as if she'd fallen into an icy lake and drowned. I shivered in horror.

I heard Marta's breath come out in a rush. "Systems nominal. Life signs stable." I swiveled, and her relieved smile took several kilos off of my heart.

"I'll check the others," Fareedh said. "It looks like this deck is *simit*-shaped, without partitions. Just a bunch of cryogenic beds in a ring around the axis. They packed it for maximum occupancy, which makes sense for a colony ship. There must be more than a thousand people sleeping in this room."

The view through his holo became a blur as he leapt toward the far wall. Pinky remained at the girl's side.

"Everything okay, Pinky?" I asked.

He was silent for a moment. Then in a curiously flat voice, he said, "She looks like you."

I licked my lips, wordless.

"She'll be okay," Marta said reassuringly. "Can you help Fareedh check the other beds?"

Another pause. Then the holo view jerked up. "Rodger dodger," he said, exactly as before.

"She looks like you."

They picked their way from bed to bed, Fareedh doing a random sampling, Pinky making a deliberate spiral course from the first one. Frozen faces loomed momentarily in their displays. They were all kinds: old, young, and middle-aged, skin tones and facial features going through all the natural and some unnatural gradations. They were wearing what looked like a thin white shift, though it was hard to tell what the original color had been. Everything was overlaid by a fine frost.

As the number of confirmed living occupants grew, Marta's report shortened to a terse "nominal" for each. I lost count after 30, and we all started to breathe more easily. It looked like the deck was full of living, if sleeping, people.

"Oh no..." I heard Marta say. I turned. Sirena had drifted close to her and floated up a couple of feet off the deck to look over her shoulder.

"What is it?" Peter reflexively put a hand on her shoulder.

Fareedh answered for her. "There's a red light third from the left in the headboard," he said. "I thought that was what it meant. This one didn't make it."

I looked back at the Window and saw a face filling the display. The man in the bed, tight dark curls framing an expressionless narrow face marked by a sharp nose and full lips, looked no more alive or dead than the rest of them.

"Are you sure?" I asked. "How can you tell?" I turned back to face Marta, feeling that unpleasant tingle along my spine.

"In cold sleep, life's processes are virtually stopped, but not completely. The report I got shows flat lines on all indicators."

"Could it be the machine?" Sirena asked.

"No," said Fareedh. "The error-check came out clean."

"I didn't mean the machine is misreporting. I mean, did the bed kill him?"

Marta shook her head. "It's 'Saelim's Reaction', I think. It affects maybe one in 10,000. Freezing people is a balancing act involving a lot of different processes. Sometimes a sleeper is less tolerant to one of them."

I heard Pinky's voice, soft and toneless, "Congratulations, Mehmet Agha. You're our lucky winner." Mehmet Agha was no one in particular; the name meant 'random person.'

It wasn't a joke in good taste, and Pinky didn't deliver it with his usual enthusiasm, but I understood the message. In a group of cold sleepers this size, we were bound to find one who didn't make it. With luck, he would be the only one.

Marta, as if reading my thoughts, added, "The longer someone's in cold sleep, the more chance a Saelim's Reaction can be fatal. I don't know how long these people have been here, but they can't be left like this indefinitely. The incidence rate can go up to one in a thousand if left too long."

That'd mean nearly a dozen dead.

"Is it a matter of minutes?" I wanted to know.

"No, no. Months. We're okay right now."

I exhaled and slumped back in my chair. "Okay. Fareedh, Pinky, I think Level 16's pretty well mapped. Want to head down and check the others out?"

"Yeah," I heard one of them say, I don't know which.

Level 15 was a twin to 16, a dark and airless chamber with beds spaced a meter apart all the way from the central shaft to *Émilie*'s hull, more than 60 meters away. I made some quick calculations based on the distribution of the beds; there had to be around two thousand sleepers on each deck. That meant five decks crammed with colonists. I wondered what the other eleven were used for. Ship's infrastructure, controls and cargo, I guessed. There would have to be farm equipment and earth movers and such, not to mention enough food for everyone to last until the crops were in. Unless this was just the first of many ships, but then you'd think they'd have started with supplies first and a small outpost. For some reason, they'd done it all in one go.

Again, Fareedh and Pinky went in their favored patterns, the former making seemingly random leaps according to some algorithm he'd come up with, and Pinky more methodically working his way around closer to the axis. They worked in silence; all I could hear from their comms was Fareedh's breathing—Pinky's respiration doesn't make sound unless he wants it to. Marta went through the bed feeds without comment. After several minutes of no report, I relaxed into my chair. No news was good news.

My stomach made a complaining noise, somewhere between a gurgle and a squelch. I straightened out, flushing slightly.

"Hungry?" Sirena asked.

"Yeah," I said. "I guess it's been a fair stretch since breakfast." I thought about asking someone to bring me a snack, then realized that, of everyone on the bridge, I probably had the least to do. Except for Sirena, maybe, but I wasn't going to ask *her* to bring me food.

Getting to my feet, I asked, "I'm going to hit the wardroom. Anyone want anything?"

Peter whipped around as if stung by a biterbug, eyes wide. "For the love of infinity, coffee please."

Which in his case meant Maker-made and triple sugar. Easy enough. "Sirena? Marta?"

"I'm fine, darling."

Marta simply shook her head, eyes focused on her *sayar*.

I looked at the Maker, lips pursed in indecision. What did I want? The Maker could produce almost anything as long as it was in its memory, and we'd all put in dozens of recipes since we'd started flying. It still couldn't create anything super fancy, and the presentation left something to be desired, but if I wanted a kofte pita, a macaroni casserole, or just a brioche and jam, the Maker could print it up for me in a jiffy. All the magic blue box needed was the raw material, and we still had plenty of that, in part because of *Majera's* efficient recycling systems. I smiled ruefully. That kind of toilet-to-table system made some people squeamish. For Pinky, it was just fodder for endless jokes. "I'll have what you had." Or, "I hope you enjoy—I put a lot of myself into this."

I decided on a salad; I wanted something crunchy and healthy-ish. There were a few types, but I just went for a minced medley of vegetables. It came out looking pretty good, though there was a regularity to the shape of the yellow, green, and red bits that betrayed that they'd been Made. As an afterthought, I asked for a blob of vinaigrette, which the Maker gave me in a glistening little sphere. I plucked it and dropped it on top, and it spread over the salad in a spiral.

For a moment, I considered getting my *cezve*, the metal pot I brought with me everywhere, to make real coffee in. I decided that the taste would clash. Instead, I checked the cupboard to see what kind of tea we had, preferring what I can brew myself to what the Maker produces. Which reminded me to ask the Maker for Peter's coffee while I set the kettle boiling for the tea.

By the time I'd gotten back, Fareedh and Pinky were on Level 14, at first glance identical to the levels above it. One difference was obvious, though. Mixed in the sea of green and blue lights were spots of red. I licked my lips and sat down heavily, placing the salad bowl and tea cup into custom depressions on the panel.

"Do those lights mean what I think they mean?" I asked.

"Checking now," Fareedh replied.

I heard an odd rhythmic sound, and when I swiveled, I saw it was Marta's finger tapping against her *sayar*. Her normally cheerful features were tight.

Pinky's voice came in, "The ones near me are fine." His display showed a young woman, frosted over, before blurring with motion as he ambled to the next bed.

"These aren't," Fareedh said. "There's a cluster here," I heard him clear his throat, "The beds are in factory default. They…" As his display turned to the nearby cryo chamber, I caught a glimpse of something inside—not frosty white but a riot of black, blue, and green glistening with moisture. The display suddenly winked out.

"Fareedh?" I called out.

"I'm here. I… I don't think you want to see this."

"What's going on, Fareedh?"

I felt a hand on my shoulder and I jerked in response. It was Sirena, floating behind my and Pinky's seats. "They're dead, aren't they?" she asked.

"Very."

"How long?"

"I'm not a doctor," Fareedh said, his voice low and controlled. "Weeks, at least."

I shuddered, the image of the corpse in all the colors of decay burned into my brain. "How many?"

"Counting now." A little later, "Fourteen in this group. There are other clusters I need to check out."

I turned to Peter. "How could this have happened?"

He shrugged his wide shoulders. "A power surge, maybe?" He looked doubtful. Then his expression cleared. "Hey, Fareedh. Is there any discoloration in the deck or ceiling?"

Fareedh's display came to life, the view swinging up and down. A cone of light illuminated the ceiling, then the floor. They looked normal to me.

"Hold it there," Peter said. He stared at the patch of deck between two beds, a crease appearing between his fair eyebrows. "Kitra, I know they're not done with this level, but I want to see what the next one below looks like."

"Yeah. Yeah, go for it." I felt an unpleasant surge inside me, adrenaline kicking in. I was certain I wasn't going to like what we found.

Fareedh's display became a rush of lights and shadows as he flew toward the axis. Pinky seemed not to have heard, continuing his methodical circuit between the rings of cryo units closest to the central shaft. He showed up in Fareedh's display once he'd landed near the hatch, a strange starfish shape humping its way forward.

"Pinky? You coming?"

"Yes," he said. But he continued on his path, methodically moving from bed to bed, his display swinging left and right as he peered in each glowing chamber. It wasn't until he'd completed the circle that took him fully around the axis, that he turned to face Fareedh, gave a jaunty wave of one of his five legs, and followed him into the shaft.

"What was that about?" Sirena whispered into my ear. I shook my head. I'd never seen him do that before. Or... had I? A memory fluttered deep in the back of my mind, buried under the years. I snatched for it, but it fled.

"Lucky thirteen," I heard Pinky say. In Fareedh's display, his fingers worked the hatch lock on the next level down, and it slid open to reveal darkness followed by the galaxy of lights. There were clusters of red, too, and to my eyes, they seemed more prominent.

"Can you check out the location directly under where you were on the last level?" Peter asked.

Fareedh's display was already a blur. "On it," he responded.

Pinky, on the other hand, began his circuit again, walking gingerly on magnetic soles between the two innermost rings, his display swinging back and forth. The frigid faces looking up from their beds were a reassuring contrast to the field of red lights looming in Fareedh's display.

"You're right," Fareedh said as he landed. "There's at least a couple dozen here, all reset. And," he pointed his light at the floor, "look at that."

This time, the discoloration was obvious. A purplish sheen reflected back at the display, completely unlike the matte off-white of the rest of the deck.

"I have a suspicion," Peter said. His arms were folded.

"What is it?" Sirena asked.

"It's not a power surge, and anyway, the beds would all use broadcast power. They wouldn't be on a physical circuit, so if any went out, it should be in a random distribution, not in a cluster. Something else cut through the ship, and it's going to get bigger as you go down."

"Don't leave us in suspense," I said facing him. I realized I was literally at the edge of my seat.

"He's talking about a field rupture," Pinky's voice came over. He was still making his way forward as he spoke. "A fault at the moment of Jump-out."

Peter nodded. "Yeah. It can happen if egress happens at the edge of a planet's safe zone, especially with bigger ships." He looked at his console, calling up *Émilie's* position around the planet. A few taps of his thick fingers and a dozen ellipses ringed the planet, the colony ship a glowing point on one of them. A fuzzy green spherical shell generated by the display surrounded the world and intersected with the closest ends of the rings. "The colony ship's orbit has precessed some in the last few weeks, but you can see that the periapsis is too close for comfort. If the *Émilie* popped out right there…" he trailed off, his pale face further drained of color.

It was suddenly very cold on the bridge. I'd known that ships that tried to Jump out too close to a planet or star simply never came back to normal space. I hadn't known that the edge of the safe zone was fuzzy. Again, I resolved to lecture Pinky about his hotshot Jumps. Or maybe not. He was surrounded by evidence of the kind of thing that could happen as a result of sloppy navigation. Maybe that's why he was acting so strangely. We weren't Jumping anywhere soon. It could wait.

"Doing a rough calculation," I heard Fareedh say, "I'd guess the effect is centered on Deck 11. That should be the one just under the last colonist level, assuming 2000 beds per deck."

"Let's skip 12 and go right to it," I said, partly because I wanted to get to the bottom of this, and partly because I didn't want to have to see an increasing number of dead colonists in their beds. No, not beds; caskets. In any event, I was worried about Pinky.

Once again, Fareedh had to wait while my oldest friend completed circling the *Émilie*'s central shaft. Then they exited the hatch, tipped themselves 90 degrees so the deep shaft became a corridor again, and drifted two decks down.

The hatch to Deck 11 wouldn't respond to Fareedh's commands, either from his personal *sayar* or the door unit. It was a rectangular hatch rather than the iris types at the top of the shaft. Fareedh and Pinky slid their lights along the jams of the portal until they found the manual override, which Fareedh toggled. It still wouldn't open.

Pinky clambered onto it and anchored himself at the crease between the two panels that made up the door. I watched Pinky's fifth pseudopod slide back into his round body, the mass redistributing to his remaining four legs. He stiffened, and I heard a creak: the sound of the doors parting conveyed through the soles of his suit. Little by little, the hatch opened under the strength of Pinky's limbs until the gap was wide enough for him and Fareedh to squeeze into.

I gasped. Their lights played onto a nightmare.

It had once been the command deck, that much was clear. Instead of the wide open space of the colonist bays, this level was partitioned, the room we were looking into perhaps a tenth of the deck's total volume. Consoles and chairs were vaguely recognizable but now in twisted, tortured forms. Not a single light or indicator remained active; Fareedh and Pinky's beams were the only illumination. Everywhere their lights touched, that same purplish sheen reflected back at them.

The worst part was the bodies. They floated, half a dozen of them, too charred to even think of them as corpses. Fareedh approached one of them gingerly. Slowly rotating, it wore the remains of a uniform, a kind of coverall. It turned to face us, staring with sightless eyes, mouth hung open, its face a vacuum-dried ruin. I heard a retching sound. Peter left the bridge in a hurry.

"Bad Jump," Pinky said.

Chapter 10

Steam wafted off the cup of coffee in my left hand, the aroma registering with me off and on. The fingers of my other hand drummed an
unconscious beat on the wardroom table. I stared at the flat white expanse of the table, not really thinking about anything in particular,
not meeting the eyes of my friends. My mind was numb. A stray
thought in the back of my head noted that my bright, newly-Made
dress hadn't given anyone luck at all.

Marta gave a little cough. "I said, what are we going to do?"

"I heard," I snapped. I looked up. She didn't seem stung or upset,
just worried. "I'm sorry. It's a lot to process," I said more softly.

Fareedh and Pinky had completed their survey of the upper
decks: at least 400 of the 10,000 colonists had passed away in failed
beds. Worse still, everyone on the flight deck, all 89 of the crew, had
died at their stations. It had to be what Peter had feared. The egress
from Jump had caused the field surrounding the ship and shielding it
from the weirdness of hyperspace to buckle. Probably not for more
than an instant, but it had sent spears of destruction throughout the
ship. It was a miracle that the vessel had retained power at all. We still
weren't sure why the damage had concentrated on the flight deck or
what shape the lower decks were in.

About the only silver lining in all of this was that death must have
been quick for the crew. I didn't want to consider the fate of the sleepers whose beds had malfunctioned. There was no way to know how
long it had taken for them to die, or if they had been aware of it happening.

I started at the hand on my wrist. It was Sirena.

"Why don't we go back?" It was a suggestion, not a question.

Fareedh quirked a dark eyebrow. "Just leave them here?"

Sirena shook her head, crescent earrings chiming gently. "Of course not. I mean to get help."

"Help could be weeks in coming," Marta said. "The beds could fail while we're gone."

Peter rubbed at his chin. There was blonde stubble coming in. "That's a definite possibility. I'll see if I can set up some redundant power shunts to keep things from breaking down further." He looked up at me with a worried look. "Or I could mess up the whole thing. It's not like I'm rated to maintain systems this big."

"Maybe we should thaw them all now and get them on the planet's surface," Fareedh offered. "Provided it's safe down there." He looked at Marta.

Her forehead wrinkled as she shrugged. "I have no idea. We'd have to get some samples. Even then, it'd just be a first order survey, finding out if anything's toxic in the short term."

Fareedh's smile held no joy. "We know one thing already that's toxic in the short term."

I licked my lips. "I feel like we should ask them what they want to do."

Pinky, sitting directly across from me, raised an overlong finger. "Kitra, they're asleep. Only you talk in your sleep."

"Do not. What if we chose a representative to wake up and asked them what they wanted to do? In any event, they'd need a personal witness to complete the colony claim..." My voice trailed off and I looked down as I realized what I was saying.

But Sirena simply said, "That's a good idea, Kitra."

"You might lose the planet," Fareedh noted.

The princess shook her head. "The *Émilie* has undergone a tragedy I wouldn't wish upon anyone. We're obliged to help them. Someday, it could be Atlántida in need."

I let out a breath, glad that I could defer the final decision a little longer. I didn't want to be responsible for the fate of an entire colony. If we revived their leader, it'd be off my plate.

Marta was looking at her *sayar*, paging through some kind of list. "It would be easier if the crew had..." she swallowed then continued, "if there were members of the crew left to ask. Their rank and positions are listed in the manifest. I'm not sure how we'll find a member of the colony's government, if there even is one. There's no passenger listed as 'mayor' or anything. It's just an alphabetical list next to a cry-obed number."

"We play *duma duma dum* and pick one at random?" Pinky sug-gested.

Fareedh leaned past Peter to peer at the *sayar*. "If there are at-tached personnel files, we could do a search for key phrases. 'Civil Servant' or something."

"Right." she said, fingers already flying. She snapped in triumph. "*Napakymppi*. They're all here." She looked over at him. "You want to do some search magic on these lists?"

"My pleasure," he drawled, leaning back with his *sayar*. "Lessee. School information; no that's not it. Assuming the colony voted lead-ership before they left, which would make sense, it probably wouldn't be tied to their degree. They'd want a nice mix of specialties in a town council. Ah, here's the profession list. Hmm. No mention of colonial positions. Let's see if there were folks who were in government jobs before they left." He pursed his lips back and forth. "Here we go. City Manager, Vice Mayor. Oooh..." His eyebrows rose.

"What?" Sirena and I said in unison.

"This one's latest position was, or is, 'Deputy Minister for the In-terior for Glorie'. Camille Unger." Fareedh made a flicking motion, and a holo of a face appeared above the center of the table, presum-ably Unger's. Short dark hair framed a pale, mature face with wrin-kles just coming in at the corners of the eyes. Their gender was not immediately apparent. Their expression was neutral; it was the kind of holo found in every official document ever made in the history of humanity.

"This is the one?" I asked.

Fareedh shrugged. "Good as any to start with, and better than some, I'd wager."

"Certainly better than the dead ones," Peter noted grimly.

Sirena reached across the table to put a hand on Marta's wrist. "Darling, can you safely thaw a sleeper?"

"Oh yes." Her confident expression faltered. "Well, under normal circumstances. The problem is you can't defrost in a vacuum."

Peter coughed and muttered, "Revive."

"What's that?" Marta asked, looking over at him.

His jaw was fixed. "Can we say 'revive' instead of 'thaw' or 'defrost'? They're people, not... not dinner." I nodded slightly, realizing it had been bothering me, too.

Marta blinked, then colored. "Yes, of course. I'm sorry."

"S'okay."

A moment of silence, then Marta continued, "Anyway, there needs to be air for a revival."

"Can we bring Unger's bed on board?" Sirena asked.

Peter tapped the table, shaking his head. "Those beds are going to be connected to the ship's power network. We don't have a good way of keeping one with consistent power if we want to move it to the ship." He swallowed. "Even a flicker might mess things up. I'd want as few variables as possible."

"Well, we certainly don't have enough air on *Majera* to fill an entire deck," I said. "What if we made some kind of tent around one of the beds?"

Marta nodded. "Yes, that's what I was thinking. That should be doable." She frowned. "Of course, that's assuming the cryo systems are functioning properly. It's a largely automatic sequence. But if things go sour during the process..." She spread out her hands in uncertainty.

"Don't borrow trouble," Pinky said. Then he turned his nub of a head so his eyespots were facing me. "Sorry. That's your line, Kitra."

I smiled weakly. "That was my mom's line. But yes. We've got enough trouble. No need to borrow more." I gave the holo a long look. "Let's go deliver The Honorable Deputy Minister the bad news. I hope..." I noted the "N" in the gender field of Unger's bio, "...they're up to hearing it."

I saw a holo video once, set on an alien world. A group of archaeologists from Earth were uncovering the tomb of an ancient leader. It was a horror show, so when they opened it, a bunch of technological traps were unleashed and they all ultimately died horrible deaths. It's an old story, of course, going back to the Egyptian tomb plunderers of the last millennium.

I felt like we were in that video, under the translucent tarp that kept in a pocket of air on the otherwise uninhabitable Level 14 of the

Émilie. A portable lamp was pasted to the apex of our makeshift dome, casting blurry shadows within and sharp ones in the vacuum outside. It was a small space, pretty tight. Fareedh, Peter, and Marta's heads all grazed the top of the bag. I was glad to be much shorter than them, though there still wasn't much room to my sides, what with the air bottle on my right and Sirena on my left.

We needed to all be here: Fareedh to monitor the ship's *sayar*, Peter to watch the power levels, me and Sirena there as the leaders of our expedition, and of course, Marta to watch over the patient. I hoped Pinky was all right back at the ship, keeping *Majera* warm. Then again, after his odd behavior last time he was on the colony ship, it was probably better for him not to be here.

Unger laid in the cryobed before me. The Minister no longer looked frozen, though the yellowish light was not flattering to the official's features. We were now an hour into the process, and no red lights had come on.

As Marta pored over the diagnostic displays, a memory came back to me in a rush, so sharp as to have a tang of immediacy: the last time Pinky had ambled in odd circles.

It was after my last trip in space as a child, the one in which I'd lost my mother. A series of shuddering hull breaches had torn *L'émissaire* apart, though not all at once—there'd been just enough time to get the children into escape pods. Mom had died trying to herd all of us in.

Pinky had been on Vatan at the time. There was a very small group of his race in Denizli, one of the first off-planet colonies. I'd never seen any of them except Pinky, who was a student in our class. He started young enough that we got over his weird shape almost immediately; the adult teachers took a bit longer. I liked him. I was at the best age to appreciate fart jokes, and Pinky was an expert at making them.

When I got back from that last trip, I guess I was in shock. The world seemed covered in a gauze filter. Nothing tasted or smelled or really pinged on my senses in any meaningful way. Uncle Yusuf wanted me to go back to school, but the doctors said I needed to get through the grief beforehand.

I didn't get through the grief. I just sat in my room, staring out the window. Existing, not feeling.

One day, I caught a glimpse of something pale moving through the garden between the rows of imported rowan trees. It stood out starkly, piggy pink against summer green. At first, I thought a farm animal had somehow gotten onto our grounds, but I didn't see how it could have gotten through the fences. The alien way it crept caught my interest. It shuffled slowly along on four legs, utterly headless. After a while, I realized there was a rhythm to its movement, almost like a dance.

There was a moment of clear view as it passed from one trunk to another, and that's when I saw the two eyespots facing in the direction of its path. I knew Pinky was a shapeshifter, but he'd always taken on a roughly human form. The fact that there was nothing else with this shape on the planet made me certain the thing in my garden was him.

By the time I had made the decision to open my window and call out to him, he had already disappeared around the corner of my house. I waited. Would he come back? Was he planning to chime the front door? I thought about getting up and meeting him there. Something kept me in my seat. Curiosity, I guess, mixed with apathy.

Pinky reappeared at exactly the same spot I'd first seen him, continuing in the same fashion. But instead of making another ring around the house, he turned and began coming straight toward me. As he moved, he tilted back onto his hind legs, his forelegs shrinking and sliding up his torso. A head appeared above his new shoulders. By the time he was just five or so meters away, he looked like a person, or at least a doll of a person with no facial features except the dark, spiral eyespots.

I got up and opened the window. I wasn't sure what to say, so I didn't say anything. He was now close enough to smell, an oddly pleasant cinnamon scent. Which was weird because I hadn't noticed that the alien had any odor before this. He held up a fingerless flipper of a hand in greeting.

"Hi, Kitra," he said. The pitch and tone were that of a child, and he was only half grown, perhaps a foot shorter than I was at the time.

"What are you doing here?" I asked.

He made a show of stretching his head half a meter to look down at his feet. "Standing."

I waited. His head shrunk back to normal proportions and he walked right up to the window. He could step over the frame and come in if he wanted.

"You didn't come back to school," he said.

"Yeah."

He looked at me for a long time without saying anything, no expression on his face. He reached forward and touched my hand.

"Your... mother and father," he said haltingly, as if struggling with the words. "They aren't here anymore?"

I could feel the numbness becoming stronger, a deliberate shield sliding up over my feelings. I shook my head.

Pinky seemed to consider this another long moment. Then he stretched out his arms. I looked at him blankly.

"We are very different," he said, "but I think we both do this." His limbs hooked at new elbows, making an open ring. "If you come inside the circle, we can both be sad together."

It took a moment for his words to register. Then, without thinking about it, I stepped over the frame onto the grass outside my window and into his arms. He closed them around me, and my cheek was on top of his head. Somehow, I'd expected Pinky to be cool to the touch, like a ball of rubber. He wasn't. He radiated heat.

No one had hugged me since I'd gotten back. Not Uncle Yusuf, who didn't hug, and I hadn't seen any of my friends. Inside Pinky's warmth, my shields vanished and everything behind them poured out in a rush. I didn't bother to hold back, couldn't have if I'd wanted to. All the grief for my lost mother, for my father who had died long before, for me, alone in the world. I bawled for ages, centuries, and Pinky held me the whole time, not saying a word.

A loud beep came from the cryobed, bringing me back to the present. I reached up to wipe the tears from my eyes and cursed silently as my fingers hit my clear helmet. I blinked rapidly instead, scattering little drops that floated as scintillating motes before evaporating. The clear surface of the casket slid into one of the sides, releasing vapor in a billow.

"This is it," Marta said. Her face glowed inside her helmet, lit by the sleep chamber. "The revival process is done. Now it's just a matter of waking up."

Sirena's chair lifted beside me as she angled herself for a better view. "How long will it take?"

Marta shrugged, turning away from Unger for the first time since she'd started working on the minister. "The life signs are nominal," she said. "There shouldn't be a coma or anything, just normal sleep."

Fareedh made a show of fumbling at his hip pouches. "I know I've got a horn in here somewhere."

"Just hit your suit alarm," Peter suggested with a smirk. "That'll do it."

"Why didn't I think of that?"

A croaking sound from the bed cut the joking chatter off sharply. We all looked inside the sleep chamber to see Unger stirring, eyelids still closed but fluttering.

"Did you say something, Your Honor?" I asked.

Unger's lips quivered, then, in a clearer tone I heard, "You're speaking very loudly."

"Oh, sorry!" Marta whispered.

The minister's lips curved up in a slight smile. "It's all right. Are we there?"

Sirena and I exchanged glances, but Marta raised a warning finger before either of us could speak.

"We're here, Your Honor," she said. "How are you feeling?"

Unger clenched at the fabric of the chamber mattress. It didn't look like the result of pain, more experimental use of long-unused fingers. Eyelids fluttered open and dark eyes met first my gaze, then Marta's.

"Surprisingly good," the minister said in a mid-range timbre. "This is not my first time in cold sleep. Perhaps I am getting used to it." Unger struggled to sit up. "I seem to be caught."

"Restraining straps," Marta said. "We're still in zero gee."

The minister looked confused. "Weightless? But why?"

Marta looked uncertainly to Peter, who quickly supplied an answer, "Conserving energy, Your Honor."

Unger's eyes narrowed as they looked from Peter to Marta. "I thought we had power to spare. It's funny. I thought I knew everyone in the crew, and even most of the *Glorieux*, but your faces are not familiar to me."

I licked my lips. "Your Honor, we're not from the *Émilie*. I'm Kitra Yilmaz, skipper of the *Majera*." My voice caught. How could I explain all that had happened, or why we were there?

Unger's brows knit. "I'm confused. We did leave Hyvilma, didn't we?"

Sirena put a hand on my arm, taking charge of the conversation. "Your Honor, there is no delicate way to put this. There has been an accident on this vessel. You are in orbit about your destination, but all of the crew and hundreds of the passengers have been lost. You have our deepest condolences and sorrow."

The minister blinked, then appeared to notice the tarp enclosing the cryobed. "My God. We are in vacuum as well, aren't we? Was the ship holed?"

"No, Your Honor," Sirena continued. "An accident with the Drive, we think."

"I see. Then..." Unger seemed to be working things through. "You were sent by one of our agents to follow up on us? We must have been here for some time."

The princess shook her head, the expression perfectly visible within her transparent helmet. "We are not associated with Gloire, Your Honor."

Unger waved a hand. "Camille is fine. But you *are* a rescue team from Hyvilma?"

Peter broke in, "We're a survey ship. The *Émilie*'s been here for 27 weeks, according to the ship's log."

"I see," Unger said again, aged features pale. "Then it is only dumb luck that you found us."

"Not luck," Marta said, touching a hand lightly to Unger's shoulder. "Everything's connected."

The silence stretched. I opened my mouth to ask the minister what we should do next, but they beat me to it. "There is a lot to take in and much to decide." A growling sound came from Unger's midsection, and the minister smiled faintly. "Perhaps decisions are better made on a full stomach."

Marta nodded. "Of course. You must have been completely

empty before they put you in. Why don't we get you back to our ship?"

"But I don't—" the minister was interrupted by Fareedh holding up a spare space suit, one of the shapeless utility kinds that didn't need to be fitted to an individual. "Ah. You've thought of everything."

Almost everything. Where was the minister going to stay? My first thought was to give up my cabin and bunk with Pinky, but the idea of a minister sleeping in the space my dirty underwear had been in felt disrespectful. And I certainly wasn't going to offer Consuelo's old berth in Sirena's room, for a number of obvious reasons. Actually, it made sense to bung something together in the starboard cargo bay. It was mostly empty this far into the trip, and bigger than any stateroom. It was a good solution, though things would get crowded quickly if we had to wake too many more people up.

Fareedh unstrapped Unger, offered the suit, and discreetly turned around. We followed Fareedh's example, giving a semblance of privacy to the minister. There was the sound of fabric slipping over limbs and a helmet being dogged. At last, we heard Unger's slightly muffled voice say, "I'm ready. Let's go see your ship."

Chapter 11

The minister looked more fragile once out of the bed. Clad in a white jumpsuit Peter had produced from the Maker, Unger looked like a hospital outpatient. Even sitting in the plush brown chair at the head of the table, Unger leaned forward heavily, the one gee field clearly a strain. I'd offered to reduce the gravity onboard *Majera*, but both Marta and Unger had argued against it — the former for health reasons and the latter probably out of pride.

The old official still had dignity. It carried through in their commanding tone and polished gestures. The minister seemed quite content to let me run the show, though, waving the thought aside when I tried to defer to rank and age.

Peter gave a more complete rundown of the damage the *Émilie* had suffered. The ship's fusion reactor was operational but with alarming occasional power surges; he didn't want to strain it by maneuvering the ship or turning on ship-wide gravity unless absolutely necessary. The ship's air supply was gone. He still wasn't sure why since the hull seemed to be airtight. Worse yet, there was no air in the *Émilie*'s reserve tanks. It was like something, or someone, had deliberately drained it all. He still hadn't inspected the Drive deck, but it was completely severed from the power grid.

Most of the cryosleep units were functioning, their inhabitants still alive. As long as the *Émilie*'s power held out, they would be okay. Which meant they were safe for anywhere from a matter of years to just weeks. Of course, the longer the colonists stayed in cryosleep, the greater the chance that some of them wouldn't wake up.

"It's really up to you, Your Honor," Peter said, wrapping up. "But you're going to need help. The *Émilie*'s a hulk as is. Maybe you could dispatch a message back to Gloire?"

"That won't work," Unger said with a shake of the head. "There's no one to send it to."

"What do you mean?" Sirena asked. Her chair floated close by Unger's left side.

"It may well be that Gloire as we knew it no longer even exists," the minister said gravely. "The planet we come from orbits close around a red sun prone to flare activity. We hadn't known that when we settled the system, centuries ago. The star had been in a quiet phase." Unger looked at me with bleak dark eyes. "Over the last 20 years, it's gotten progressively worse. It was a statistical certainty that the planet would become uninhabitable."

Pinky cocked his head in a deliberate mimicry of human curiosity. "Since it orbits a red sun, isn't Gloire a one-face world like, say, Punainen?" he asked.

Unger blinked. *It speaks*, I could almost hear running through the minister's mind. It was probably a good thing Pinky hadn't been at the revival; that would have been a lot to take in on top of everything else. Virtually no one in the inner half of the Empire had seen one of Pinky's people.

To Unger's credit, recovery was almost instantaneous. "No. It has a resonance with its sun such that it rotates thrice for every two orbits. Otherwise, yes, we could have theoretically holed up on the night side, though I don't know how long we could have lasted anyway in a frozen waste. It's a moot point. We had to get off the planet, and soon. All of us."

Marta was taken aback. "Wait. You mean the *Émilie* is carrying the entire population of Gloire?"

Unger nodded. "Yes."

I resisted the urge to whistle with the realization. The 10,000 souls on board the *Émilie* weren't colonists. They were *refugees*.

"Begging your pardon, Your Honor," Fareedh said quietly, "but isn't that putting all your eggs in one basket? Couldn't you have applied to the government for aid and resettled your people elsewhere, even if just temporarily?"

The minister's lips curled in a joyless smile. "I'm sure there would have been planets more than happy to take us in. Some of us, anyway. But the Empire prefers homogeneity. It doesn't want incipient nation-states on any of its planets, especially of Midworld stock. We would have been deliberately scattered. Oh, the *people* of Gloire might survive, but Gloire would be dead. We didn't struggle for centuries on a difficult planet just to suffer a diaspora."

Fareedh nodded, but he kept his expression neutral. He didn't look convinced. "But why launch everything at once?" he asked. "Why didn't you establish an outpost first? As things stand, you don't even have an established claim on the planet."

Unger took a moment before answering Fareedh. "We did not scout this world ourselves. The information was sold to us, and I cannot name the source. In any event we had neither the time nor the resources to precede the *Émilie*. As it was, we were lucky to get it so quickly."

Dark eyes that abruptly looked decades older cast down on the table. "We were in a hurry. This planet was ideal, and it was only a matter of time before someone else with an eye toward colonization found it." Unger looked up at Sirena, a grim smile playing on their thin lips. "I don't suppose you were just doing astronomical research for a university?"

"I'm afraid not, Your Honor," Sirena said softly.

"No, I didn't think so. Well then..." Unger looked down at the table again.

"We'll make sure all of your people are safe," Marta said firmly. "Whatever it takes. We can take you back to Hyvilma with as many sleepers as we can carry. You can apply for aid from there."

I opened my mouth. That was a big promise to make, certainly a commitment we shouldn't make without Sirena's input.

But Fareedh was already adding, "Yeah, there's a cruiser stationed at Hyvilma. I bet they could transport your people back there. Might take a few Jumps, but it's a big ship. Plus there's lots of room on the planet; they'd probably let you stay until you worked things out." Great. Now we were volunteering the Navy, too.

"We'll be imperial refugees out at the edge of space," Unger was saying. "And penniless on top of that. It cost virtually the entire wealth of Gloire to purchase and equip the *Émilie*."

"You'll be alive," Fareedh noted.

Unger stiffened then relaxed, gaze flickering to him. "Yes, I'm sorry. Instead of lamenting, I should be grateful. I could as easily have never woken up, and you have been more than generous." The minister stared a long moment at the glowing schematic of the crippled *Émilie*.

"So close," Unger whispered.

Fareedh's room hadn't changed much since the last trip. His tiny cabin, ceiling just a few centimeters above his head when he stood, felt bigger with the geometric sprawls and physical hangings he'd put up. Their effect wasn't anything like hyperspace; the patterns and colors on the wall were relaxing rather than bewildering.

I sat on his futon, gathering my legs beneath me, and pressed back against the wall. A mug of tea warmed my cradling hands, the spicy aroma tingling my nose. The pillows and sheet were different. I remembered them being a dizzying array of clashing colors. Now, they were a pale green, an island of solidity in contrast to the infinity of the walls. It was all very soothing.

It was what I needed. I wasn't at all sure about how things were going.

I glanced over at Fareedh sitting in the room's only chair, strumming a battered guitar. It was acoustic and maybe an antique. He looked down at his fingerings, heavy eyelashes hiding his dark eyes. Long hair curled unbound around his shoulders. He hadn't asked me why I'd stopped by, and I hadn't offered more than a "hello." We just sat in companionable silence. Fareedh was really good for that.

It wasn't that I didn't want to talk. I just didn't know how to start. A dozen different openings came to mind, none of which felt right. I still hadn't processed my thoughts, and I was afraid of airing them. They felt wrong, selfish.

But if I didn't talk to someone, the thoughts and feelings would keep seething.

At last I said, "It's going to take a month to get back here. At least."

"That's true."

"That's assuming getting help is as quick as making a couple of calls."

He looked up at me and nodded, fingers still sliding over strings.

"I mean, I want to help…"

Fareedh cocked his head slightly.

*I glanced over at Fareedh sitting in the room's only chair,
strumming a battered guitar.*

I looked down. "It's just… Sirena hired us to find a planet for her. Now we're committed to helping Unger." I licked my lips. "It's not that I don't want to help. They *need* help."

"But."

The words tumbled out, "I feel like a failure. We've found what may be the perfect planet, *again*, and now we're leaving it behind. By the time we get back, someone else may have staked a claim. Or Unger might even argue that they've satisfied *their* claim."

"Shouldn't they get that chance?" he asked mildly.

"We're supposed to be working for Sirena, aren't we?"

"Have you talked to her?"

"No. Not yet."

Fareedh rested the guitar on his bare knees and leaned forward. "Do you think Marta and I spoke out of turn? Offering to help Unger without consulting you?"

I let out a breath. "No. No, of course not. It's the right thing to do." Lord knows we would have been happy to have been rescued after we'd ended up in the middle of nowhere on our first Jump.

"I'm just impatient, I guess."

"And afraid of disappointing a princess again."

Bullseye. "A little, yeah."

His lips twitched into a wry smile. "You could always flit down and grab a handful of dirt. Maybe plant a flag. I'm sure Pinky could make something appropriate. Then our claim would be uncontestable."

I snorted a little then let out a sigh. "I know you're not serious. You saw Unger's face. Devastated. I couldn't do that." I found I couldn't meet Fareedh's gaze, so I looked into my lap instead. "I'm terrible, Fareedh. Selfish. These people need help and I'm upset about losing a few weeks' time. "

"You're not terrible. If you were, you wouldn't be talking about it. It's okay to be disappointed."

I wiggled my toes and said nothing.

"You can leave the decision to Sirena if you want. Either way, things'll work out."

"I wish I had your confidence," I said, looking up at him.

He didn't answer, but abruptly he smiled, as if at some internal joke. He picked up the guitar again, and music filled the space that words had vacated.

After a while I asked, "What is that you're playing? It's nice."

He smiled, his eyes focused on his fingering. "Just a poem I'm trying to set to music."

"Yours?"

Fareedh nodded, sliding from one chord to another and then back. I waited a moment. "Can I hear it?"

He looked down with a slight flush to his brown cheeks before meeting my gaze. His dark eyes flashed wider in an expression I always found appealing.

"If you like." He took a deep breath, eyes closed, then began to play.

> *Planets on a cosmic curve*
> *Endless black without a sound*
> *Circling round without a swerve*
> *Solar bound...*
>
> *Pool of water, clear and green*
> *Ripples leap toward the shore*
> *Sheltered safe by arms of sand*
> *Ever safe and sound.*

Fareedh's voice was surprisingly light, almost lilting, a contrast to his mellow speaking voice. The instrumentation underneath was beautiful and his fingering complex. I wondered why I'd never seen him perform back at our old hangout, Le Fontiére; he was at least as good as any act I'd heard there. I closed my eyes and listened as the rhythm and chords changed, marking a bridge.

> *When the way is lost, with chaos rife*
> *A beacon shines in through the night*

And then to an energetic chorus...

> *For the wayward souls*
> *For the tempest tossed*
> *There is always you.*

In the desperate hours
When the hope's devoured
There is always you.

The chords returned to their original progression, but now the tempo was livelier.

Stream of chicklings, path unsure
Wandering here then waddling there
Just one call will set them straight
Brought to firmer ground.

Bird caught in a violent breeze
Clouds blot out the endless sky
Wings are calmed by quiet strength
Lost, but now she's found.

Strumming hard now, Fareedh looked up at me as he went to the second bridge.

When the stars are gone and space is cold
A single voice gives hope to hold.

At the map's frontier
When the way's not clear
There is always you.

We'll get back again
There'll be happy end
All because of you.

His fingers went from strumming to picking, as he repeated the last line:

All because of you.

Fareedh put the guitar down in his lap. "It's not great," he said. "I'm still working on the lyrics, but... you get the idea."

I shook my head with a little laugh. "That can't be me you're singing about."

"It is. At least, how I see you."

I tugged at my toes. I could feel the flush in my cheeks. "I'm nothing special. Just, you know, one of the team."

Fareedh put down his instrument and came up to the futon. He was about the same height kneeling as me sitting. Fareedh didn't say anything; he just put his hands on mine and leaned forward. My stomach jumped and there was a loud thudding in my ears. It was clear what was going to happen next, and I realized that I wanted it, too. And then we were kissing.

It was nice, not hard or aggressive. He was actually a lot more tender, more tentative than I'd thought someone as experienced as him would be. I leaned into the kiss, enjoying being so close to someone again. Fareedh's gentleness was different, nice, but I had to get used to it, restrain myself. My experience mostly came with Marta, who didn't so much kiss as engulf you. What would it have been like to kiss Marta this way, I wondered, and that thought was nice, too. For a moment, I had a pleasant double vision behind my closed eyes, feeling Fareedh, remembering Marta.

My kiss faltered. Thinking of Marta brought back memories of what happened last trip, when Marta and I had... a moment... which left things awkward with me and her for weeks.

Then Fareedh slid his fingers gently against mine, and for a second, I wasn't thinking about anything but his lips, his scent. He was warm and nice and close, and he felt wonderful. My fingers slid up his thin arms.

And stopped. The eager excitement in my stomach went acidic, and the wiser part of my brain, or maybe just the frightened one, put on the brakes. I gripped Fareedh's arms gently and drew back from him.

His eyebrows rose in concern. "Sorry. I guess I've wanted to do that for a while."

He looked so hesitant and vulnerable, totally un-Fareedh-like. I couldn't help smiling as I put curled fingers to the side of his face. "You're pretty great, Fareedh," I said.

He took a breath, eyes locked on mine. "But?"

I shook my head. "No 'but.' Just… let me think about things, okay? This all came on so quickly." I laughed. "I'm not used to people composing songs about me."

"You did ask."

"Hah. You kept teasing me with the song until I had to ask."

He smiled and looked a bit more like Fareedh again. "Maybe."

I looked at him quietly for a moment, then leaned forward to hug him. His arms folded around me, and my chin was on his shoulder. I said into his ear, "This isn't a brush off, I swear."

His voice came back, "This doesn't have to be a thing. I don't want to make you uncomfortable."

"I'm not," I said, not entirely truthfully.

He gave me a final squeeze and now he was drawing back from me, but he took my hand and clasped it. "Take your time. You've got things on your mind, and first and foremost, I'm your friend and your programmer. Whatever happens."

It took a few blinks to clear my eyes. "I appreciate that, Fareedh." I brought my legs out from under me to step off the futon. They were all pins and needles once I got to a stand, and I grabbed Fareedh's shoulder to steady myself. He put his hand over mine and we remained like that quietly for a moment. Then I flipped my hand to give his a parting squeeze and excused myself. I did *not* run back to my room, close the door and scream.

I walked.

My cabin wasn't any bigger than Fareedh's, so it didn't afford much space for pacing. I did the best I could, kicking the used laundry out of the way as I walked. My mind was still whirling. What was going on? And why was I so worried? This wasn't like what had happened with Marta. Fareedh wasn't with anyone. This wasn't a one-off encounter motivated by stress. At least, I assumed that. It takes time to compose a song, and he said he'd wanted to kiss me for a long time.

Which sort of blew me away. Why me of all people? Fareedh was handsome and popular. I'd seen the way others had swooned around him, and he hadn't had to do much more than flash his eyes or make a smooth, low-voiced quip. Me… I was just… me. Brash, dragging people into danger, nothing special to look at. How could he be serious? Of course, I never quite understood what Marta was doing with me either, and she'd been the most attractive girl in school.

I stopped pacing for a moment, the fingers of my right hand rubbing together. What if he *was* serious? Lord, what if he was! Did I really want to open up another can of radioactives by dating someone in the crew? And *now* of all times?

I stopped myself, shook my head and laughed aloud. I was skipping the most important question: did I want to go out with him at all?

Okay. Calm down. Deep breaths. No need to get excited. Take Fareedh's interest as genuine. Evaluate the situation rationally.

I sat down on my bed with a whuff, palms backward behind me. My lips quirked upward as certain memories came to me. Fareedh pulling me up out of the water at the shore on Jaiyk. Offering me that fossil at the Hotel Hyvilma. The uncertain, haunted look he wore last trip when he told me why our ship's *sayar* had malfunctioned. How cool and put together he'd looked when Peter first introduced me to him two years ago. His laid-back pose when he convinced Peter to join the *Majera* crew. The way his lips felt against mine.

That brought a shiver, and I folded my arms around myself, feeling the hairs fluffed up on top of goosebumps. It had been a nice kiss.

Fareedh was a good friend, and smart, and—no two ways about it—sexy as anything. Why not?

I hadn't ever really considered going out with him. I'd enjoyed his attentions, and I certainly liked him. Even loved him, at least the way I loved Peter and Pinky. But physical reactions aside, now that I was thinking about it, now that it was really happening, some part of me was holding back. Which was weird. When Marta had first asked me out, years ago, there'd been no hesitation.

Was it me? Or something wrong with Fareedh? Maybe it was just the situation. This really wasn't a great time.

I chewed on my lip. Yes, that was probably it. First the Puritans, and then the *Émilie*. Having to choose between Sirena and Unger, between job obligation and moral duty. Weeks and weeks of tense waiting, and now more weeks of waiting before us. With all that hanging over me, I wasn't in a place to make a decision like this. I needed to walk things back, shivers or no shivers.

I felt the release that comes with a decision firmly made, and it came so strongly that I knew I was making the right choice. There was plenty of time. Fareedh was a good guy. He'd understand. And it wasn't like I was saying no forever. Just pausing things. We could try again when we got back to Hyvilma, or maybe after we found Sirena's world.

I let out a relieved sigh. Well, best to tell him now so things didn't marinate too long. I reached for my *sayar*. My eyes widened. It was glowing — Fareedh was calling *me*. How about that? Maybe he'd come to the same conclusion on his own.

I tapped at the device. "That was quick!" I said. "Listen, I was thinking..."

Then I saw that Fareedh wasn't alone; Peter had wormed his way into the display.

"Kitra," Peter said, "we've got a problem. Meet us on the bridge?"

When I got there, Marta was at her station as well as Peter and Fareedh. The Window displayed a full view of the *Émilie*, tracing the tendrils of power as they snaked through the levels of the ship. It seemed to me that they were brighter now, and the damage on Deck 11 was even more apparent as a jagged, star-shaped gap in the web.

"What's going on?" I asked.

Fareedh and Peter exchanged a quick look. Peter said, his voice pitched high with worry, "I think I broke something on the *Émilie*. I was tapping the grid points remotely when I noticed what was happening."

"It wasn't you, Peter," Marta said. "I keep telling you."

"So I asked Fareedh since he's hooked into *Émilie's* ship's *sayar* too. He confirmed it."

"What's. Going. On?" I repeated.

Fareedh put a hand on Peter's shoulder, half comfort and half restraint. "Kitra, the master sequence for the cryobeds has been triggered. They're all set to begin the revival process in about eleven hours."

My mouth opened, lips pursed to form words. Nothing came.

"I'm not sure how the safety protocols got overridden," Fareedh was saying, as if from a great distance. "Maybe the ship's sensors got confused. I haven't had a chance to figure it out."

"Kitra," Marta said urgently. "We've got to do something. There's no air on the *Émilie*."

Marta's words echoed through my head, pushing out everything else. The worries about losing a colony candidate for Sirena. About finding a home for Unger's people. About Fareedh. Marta. None of that meant anything anymore.

In less than half a day, ten thousand refugees were going to wake up, gasp.

And die.

Chapter 12

All sound had gone away. I was in a bubble of endless time, strangely calm, numb. There was just the pulsing of my heart, the rasp of my breath, in and out, in and out. I stared blankly at the display above my seat, the unfocused digits blinking from purple to green and back again. The display was the most interesting thing in the world. The moment stretched…

The bubble popped and reality came back in a whoosh: the jabber of my friends, the flat white of the deck, the slightly sharp tang of the air, the hiss of the vents. It was like a switch had been flicked in the back of my brain.

I ran a hand through my hair and stepped forward, jabbing at my panel. The ship's klaxon rang out, cutting off the conversation mid-sentence. I let the siren run for a few seconds before turning it off.

"We need everyone in on this," I explained. Fareedh gave me the ghost of a smile and nodded.

Pinky was the first onto the bridge, rubbery limbs flailing. I don't think I'd ever seen him move so fast. Unger staggered in shortly after. Sirena was the last to arrive, her hair dripping into her grav chair. She only wore a towel around her shoulders. We five of the crew took our seats to make room for the others in the small area.

"What's going on?" Unger asked. The minister had serious bed head and was blinking blearily.

"Something happened," I said in a rush. "Everyone on the *Émilie* is waking up in less than twelve hours. We've got to figure out something before then." Unger's mouth dropped open as I continued. "Minister, do you have any idea what could have caused this? Was the revival set to a specific deadline or something?"

Unger was lost in thought for a moment, or maybe just dazed. At last, "No, I shouldn't think so. Waking up is something that should only have been triggered manually by the crew."

"Who aren't around to give such a command," Pinky noted. "Given how beaten up the crew deck was, I suppose something could have faulted, though."

"Yeah," Peter said. "Right after I started surveying the ship." His voice was agonized with guilt.

"You mean after I started probing the ship's *sayar*," Fareedh corrected.

Marta cut in, "Or after we triggered a revival sequence." Unger blanched at that.

Sirena spoke loudly to end the debate. "Maybe it was our fault. Maybe it wasn't. The people of Gloire were already dying on this ship *before* we got here, and had we not arrived, they might have all perished before anyone found them. God has a hand in these matters, too."

I found myself nodding. Blame could be assigned later, and then only for the purpose of solving problems, not to beat ourselves up. I smiled at Sirena gratefully. "First thing is to do what we can with what we have," I said, "Peter, if we spare all of the air from *Majera*, leaving us, say, an eight-day supply to Jump for help, how much can go to the *Émilie*?"

"I can tell you right now, there won't be enough to fill even a deck, let alone the whole ship," he protested.

"But how much? Half a deck's worth?" I asked.

Peter shrugged. "Maybe?"

"It's a start. That's five hundred people." I looked over at Unger, licked my lips, and said, "It'd be up to you to decide who."

Unger looked at me with haunted eyes, the wrinkles seamed even more deeply into their aged face. At last, the minister nodded. "Marta, how long do we actually have until the waking process is irreversible?"

She shook her head, disheveled curls bobbing. "I can only use your case as a model. There were four hours of diagnostics before the revival processes started."

I winced. So little time.

"There's clearly some sort of hull breach," Pinky was saying. He flushed a deeper pink in concentration. "Peter and I could set up a partition, bigger than the one we made for Unger. Also, we could have the Maker produce some kind of sheeting. Perhaps the *Émilie's* Makers are functioning, too."

"That'll take a while to set up," Peter said.

"Fareedh," I said, my voice almost pleading, "is there *any* way to delay the revival process?"

"I'm still not even sure why it's happening, but I can go into the system and see what I can find." He was already throwing displays up on his console, eyes darting over them.

I bit my lip and thought. The easiest solution would be to just take *Émilie* where the air was — down to the planet. But the giant, ungainly ship had probably been assembled in orbit from pieces floated from dirtside. I doubted it could survive reentry, much less a padless landing. Not to mention I wasn't sure the *Émilie's* antigravity was even working. No, it simply wasn't an option.

A thought dawned on me. "Maybe I could bring some air up from the planet in one of the gigs. I bet we could at least fill the rest of a deck with a load. That's another five hundred. There might be time for more trips, too."

Marta leaned half out of her seat. "I'd have to go with you. We don't even know if the air down there is breathable. And if it is, it may still be unsafe with pathogens."

"Yeah, of course. Alright then." I turned on a heel, ready to suit up and get moving as fast as I could.

Sirena stopped me with a hand on my shoulder.

"Wait, Kitra." She looked at me intently, beads of water glistening on her. "If we had another pilot, we could fly both shuttles and perhaps fill another deck in time, provided the air is breathable." Sirena inclined her head to Unger, "Your Grace, though the crew of the *Émilie* is no longer with us, are there pilots among the refugees?"

"Y-yes. I can think of a few off the top of my head."

"Then we can move the mobile air partition to one of them. If we can wake them without accelerating the cycles for the rest."

I looked at Fareedh, who raised his eyes from his work to meet mine, then Sirena's. "I don't know what triggered everyone's cycle in the first place, but while I can't isolate a bed power-wise, I can probably set up a firewall to the ship's *sayar* to prevent further instructions going back and forth." He whistled through his teeth. "I should have thought of that before."

"I see only one flaw in the plan," Pinky noted, heavy fingers interlaced. "Kitra is taking our only medically trained crewmember with her."

Sirena arched an eyebrow. "*I'm* a doctor," she said blandly.

I imagined I could hear all of us blinking in unison. "You never told me that!" I exclaimed.

The princess smiled slightly. "You never asked, darling."

I looked at her incredulously, revising my estimate of her age upward. I'd thought that she couldn't be much older than us. Then again, there was no reason Sirena couldn't be as old as 50, especially as a noble with access to the best anti-aggs.

"Then, Your Highness, I think that'd be a great idea," I said.

"It would be my pleasure."

I took a deep breath, my heart racing. Then I got up, looked at Marta, and said, "Let's go."

The two identical ship's boats moored to the top deck of the *Émilie* were about the same size as the *Majera*, but completely different on the inside. They were strictly interplanetary ships, and even calling them that was stretching a point. Though they had big engines and power plants, they had neither the Jump Drives nor the giant fuel tanks needed for a trip across the stars. Instead, they were almost all cargo bay. That made sense if the *Émilie* wasn't designed for landing. The *Glorieux* had probably planned to shuttle people and equipment planetside, leaving the main ship in orbit. The *Émilie* would have been used to export goods to other worlds in the frontier once the settlement had become productive. If the colony failed, the *Émilie* would be there to take the refugees somewhere else. Of course, the big ship wasn't going anywhere now.

I pinged the first gig with a command from my *sayar*. If it was as messed up as its mother ship... but the shuttle responded immediately. Its hatch irised open, the lock lights turning on automatically. Marta pressed in behind me as I closed the outer door and cycled the inner one, which opened onto the cargo bay. The lights snapped on here, too. The big cargo hold was virtually featureless except for the door to the pilot compartment up front and access to the rear, presumably engineering, section. There were grooves at regular intervals along the floor that might have been recessed seats or cargo hooks. I'd have to play around with the controls to know.

The passage to the gig's bridge also had a working airlock. Better still, when I got the inner door open, I felt the whoosh of incoming pressure. That meant there was air in the control room, and there weren't any leaks. I wasn't going to take my suit off any time soon, especially with six hours of supply in my bottle, but it was reassuring nonetheless.

The control room was less a bridge and more just a cockpit, big enough for two seats, a Window, and a pair of small consoles. I took the left seat, and Marta weightlessly flew to the right one, easing herself down and strapping in. Thankfully, the controls looked much like that of the *Majera* – or most Imperially-licensed small craft for that matter. That was good. I'd trained on a few ships to get my piloting certificate, but they'd all been of a type. If the gig had been nonstandard, I'd have had to wait until Unger revived a sleeper. There was no time for that.

The Window and panels came to life with a press of the finger. More good news, but that just meant the batteries worked. The real test would be powering up the power plant at the back of the ship. I called up the power plant controls and looked for the pre-start diagnostic cycle.

"Is it safe?" Marta asked. I turned, and she was looking at me.

I forced a laugh. "Things have to be just right for a nuclear reactor to work at all. If there's something wrong with the plant, it won't blow up. It just won't turn on." I turned back to the controls, trying to find what I wanted in the forest of options. There. The pre-start sequence. I activated it and watched as a readout of checks sprang up, superimposed upon a glowing outline of the reactor's components. I strapped myself in, gripping the control sticks experimentally as the flood of comfortingly green text floated by.

While that was going on, I poked around the control systems some more. The shuttle wasn't equipped with internal antigravity; that was going to make reentry interesting. In fact, it didn't look like there was an antigrav engine, either. Everything was done with fusion thrust and control surfaces on the wings. I couldn't just drop down to the planet as I could in the *Majera*. I'd have to fly in. Well, I'd done that before, and in ships less aerodynamic than this one.

The plant diagnostic chimed, the reactor outline now a shimmering green. Without hesitation, I began the start-up sequence. There was immediate feedback, a thrum I felt through my suit as immense pressures built up inside the gig's reactor, a tiny star just twenty or so meters behind us. I hadn't been entirely accurate when I told Marta there was no danger of explosion. With the kind of energies compressed in the plant chamber, a serious asymmetry or fault in the reactor, and we'd go boom so fast, we wouldn't even know it. I held my breath and tried not to think about it as the temperature indicators went up higher and higher. All I could do was trust the instruments.

I tapped the armrest impatiently as the temperature and pressure plateaued. Finally, there was another chime.

"I'm heading out," I commed breathlessly to *Majera*.

"Godspeed," came Sirena's accented reply.

I pinged *Émilie*'s hangar door, which responded as readily as it had when we'd been outside the colony ship. Once again, the chamber opened to the stars. I couldn't see the planet below from here. The magnetic anchors disengaged, the gig lurching beneath my seat.

The gig's *sayar* offered to handle the maneuvers to exit *Émilie*'s hangar. I wasn't comfortable handing over control of the ship to its electronic brain given the state of *Émilie*'s ship's *sayar*, so I nudged the gig's thrusters myself, pushing us lightly from the deck and then, with another squirt of thrust, kicked us through the portal.

I thought I heard a little gasp. I looked at Marta, who had her hands on her stomach. "You okay?" I asked.

"Not used to all this jerking around in zero gee. I'll be okay." She smiled weakly. "If I make any embarrassing noises, I'll blame it on Pinky."

My helmet speakers crackled. "You know I can hear you, don't you?" came Pinky's smooth baritone.

"She knows, pal," I said. "Take it as a compliment."

"Oh, I do."

I grinned. Maybe it was whistling past the graveyard, but it was better than screaming.

Tapping at the gig's console brought up a map of the planet: a vast expanse of ocean with that single big continent. Getting there wouldn't be too difficult. Our orbit had us passing right over it. Landing was going to be the issue, especially without antigrav. I cycled through the controls and found ventral thrust ports along the bottom. I'd only made thrusted landings a few times, but as long as fuel wasn't a concern, I figured I could probably make it down okay.

But why risk landing at all? We were in a hurry. Couldn't we do a quick zoom at a few hundred meters, open up the cargo bay and let in a hold of air? No, that wouldn't work. Unlike *Majera*, which was designed to scoop gas from the outside for fuel, if I opened the gig up in the air, it'd mess up the flight profile of the ship and probably send us tumbling. It really was a no frills ship compared to mine.

"Pinky, I don't trust the programs on this tub. Can you find me a good, flat landing spot on the northern continent, somewhere with reasonable weather, and send me deorbit calculations? This is a pretty standard vessel type. It shouldn't be hard to plug in the thrust and flight profiles."

"No problem," he replied. "Let's see."

My personal *sayar* came to life, connecting to the gig's Window to throw up a display that edged aside the planet map. I watched as Pinky considered and discarded a number of potential spots until he found one he liked. "How about this?" he asked. I saw a slightly fuzzy view of a broad plain, blue-gray with distance, a couple of rivers winding through it. A bright spot appeared on the map. From the scale, it looked like the area was about ten by ten kilometers. Pinky's calculations called for a deorbiting burn in eight minutes. They also included a slight plane change right away so I could put some real separation between us and the *Émilie*.

"Looks as good as anything," I said. "You draw a good map, Pinky."

"You make me swell with pride," was the reply. He probably meant it literally.

"Making my first burn, you big balloon," I said through a smile.

Turning to Marta, I said, "This one shouldn't be bad, but make sure you're strapped in good and tight." She nodded, running hands over her harnesses and tugging. I thrustered some space from the colony ship, called a three second countdown and then lit the main engines.

About half a gee pressed against my back, and the *Émilie* receded at 5 meters per second per second, quickly dwindling to a toy, a sparkle, nothing. It was just us and the slowly spinning world below, the twilighted terminator drifting behind us. We were orbiting into the day, which was good—I wouldn't have wanted to try to navigate in the dark. Then I turned the engine off, and we were weightless again. Per Pinky's plot, we had several minutes before the next maneuver.

Marta leaned back in her chair with a sigh and stared up at the ceiling, a wistful expression on her face.

"Some birthday this turned out to be."

I blinked. It was such an incongruous thing to say, it took me a moment to process what she'd said.

"Wait, it's your birthday?"

She looked over at me and smiled a bit sadly, her curls floating freely in the almost transparent bubble of her helmet.

"My Vatan birthday, I mean. It started just an hour ago. I'm 20 years old now," she said in a rush, clearly as tense as I was. She pulled out her *sayar* in a jerk and showed me the display. There were two slowly moving chronometers, one in ship's time based on Imperial standard, and the other set to Vatan's year of 174 Vatanian days. The Vatanian side read exactly 20; the other was almost halfway between 20 and 21.

"I should have remembered," I said sheepishly.

Her laugh was almost a bark. "There are bigger things to worry about. Besides, did you remember *your* birthday?"

That caught me flat footed. Once I'd hit Vatan 17 and gotten my adult citizenship, it hadn't mattered much. Certainly not enough to have a party or anything. And now, with multiple time scales to bother with, it was just too much trouble to keep track. I should have remembered at least one of Marta's birthdays, though.

"I guess I need one of those, too," I said, pointing to her *sayar* display.

She took a deep breath, calming herself. "It's no big deal. It's just a thing of mine. I always want to know what time it is and how it relates to me. Makes me feel more connected with everything, you know?"

I nodded, remembering. When we'd been going out, Marta had never showed up 'fashionably late': not to dates or parties or anything. Peter and Marta had always been the most reliable of my friends. If they were going to be late, they'd always let me know. I'd always taken it for courtesy, but I saw now that it ran deeper than that for the two of them.

"And I hadn't wanted to make a big deal about my Imperial 20th while we were getting ready for the trip," Marta was saying.

"If it makes you feel better, we'll have a double celebration when we get back for both of your 20ths," I said.

"Oooo. I'll hold you to that."

As the minutes ticked by, I cycled through the ship's subsystems, as much out of nerves as wanting to familiarize myself with what the shuttle could do. We were probably fine. After all, Pinky's program would get us down safely to the lower atmosphere, and beyond that, an airplane was an airplane, right? That is, if the gig's ship's *sayar* didn't have some kind of problem that turned off the automatic compensators, froze a control surface in a weird position, or otherwise made itself unusable. There was no way I could fly the thing without *sayar* assistance.

"You okay?" Marta asked. She always knew when I was worried.

I laughed it off. "Oh yeah, sure." I looked at the time display. "I'm going to spin us around." A quick play of the thrusters and we were headed backward, the sun streaming past us from behind. In 58 seconds, I'd be hitting the main engine again and we'd stop orbiting. Or rather, we'd enter a new orbit, one that would, if we did nothing else, intersect very rapidly with the ground.

I mouthed a little prayer. The gig had to work. Beyond saving hundreds of lives, now I had a promise to Marta to keep.

A tap of the thrusters, and the gig pitched down about 25 degrees. Blue and white swirled below the tip of the shuttle's nose. Then another five second countdown and the engines hit hard this time. No longer just a dull rumble, the engines made a roar quite unlike anything the *Majera* created. I felt fragile, like I was sitting at the head of a zero-gee squeeze bottle that could collapse at any moment. The burn was just half a minute by the gig's chronometer, but it felt like an eternity. All at once, the engines stopped and we lurched forward into free fall again. I swung the gig around, flaring the nose up. Soon, we'd be hitting the atmosphere.

It was funny. All those little things I had been worried about had made me nervous and on edge. Now, here I was in the midst of a much bigger crisis, and I was strangely calm. Maybe it was because I had a clear course of action. I'd freak out if I had time.

The gig began reentry. At first, it barely registered: a few streamers of flame across the nose, a tiny shuddering in the control sticks. I looked over at the course display. We were coming in pretty hot. Ideally, we'd have started our burn twenty minutes earlier and had a gentle reentry path that covered half the globe. That would have minimized heating and kept deceleration gees down, too. Instead, Pinky had programmed a descent that got us down as fast as possible for a free-flying ship. It also meant we'd be pushing the tolerances of the gig. And us. Hotshotting again? No, probably just recognizing the hurry we were in.

The sticks were now shuddering constantly. I could have locked in the automatic controls, but I felt safer just having the compensators on. The gees mounted, pressing us down hard into our seats toward the deck. The gig's skin temperature gauge crept up steadily. It was over 500° K already. With leaden fingers, I made a quick *sayar* search through the gig's specs for the maximum safe temperature: 2000° K. Plenty of margin. I would have sighed in relief but my breath felt locked in my chest by four times its normal weight.

There was a flickering golden sheen over the dappled blue of the planet now, the thin gasses of the upper atmosphere blazing against the shuttle at a dozen times the speed of sound. Ahead, the continent was a fuzzy, darker mass, half hidden by clouds. I commed Pinky to let him know we were alright, but no reply came. Blocked by the ionized plasma around us, I guessed. It didn't really matter; he had to have been tracking our beacon up to the communications blackout zone. He'd see us when we were through.

If we made it. Hull temperature was up to 1000°. I struggled with the controls to keep us on the glowing glide path Pinky had provided me. The display was blurry at the edges, from the gees and the shaking.

"Just like your glider back home?" Marta gasped.

"Oh yeah. I used to go higher than this all the time," I managed to joke.

The altimeter read 70 kilometers. We were more than halfway down now and the Window was an inferno. The polarizers kicked in, reducing the glare from the blaze, and the creaking of the hull started to compete with the roar from outside conducted through the gig's skin.

"Stupid, bargain basement builders," I muttered through gritted teeth. Marta looked at me worriedly. I kept my mouth shut after that.

1500°. Should I flare the nose up further? Push the nose down? I honestly had no idea what would be the right move here. I thought furiously. If I flared up... no, that was definitely wrong. At the current air density, we'd heat up even worse and probably be knocked around like a kite in a gale. If I lowered the nose, we wouldn't decelerate as fast, and the heat would be lower. But then we might overshoot the target and have to circle back. I didn't want to take any more time than I had to.

I licked my lips and called up the atmosphere data we'd collected from *Majera*, comparing it to Pinky's flight profile. We had to be near max temperature now. Better not to take a chance. Still, I held my breath.

Another endless stretch of time with arms like lead. Then the altimeter read sixty kilometers, and the hull temperature was down to 1400°.

"We're going to make it," I heard Marta whisper.

"You betcha."

Slowly, the weight crept away from our limbs. At last, I felt almost me-massed again. I wriggled my shoulders to get the kinks out. Marta was rubbing ruefully where the straps had cut into her. At 50 kilometers, the comms crackled to life. "...in Kitra. Do you receive? We see your beacon. Come in Kitra. Do you receive?" Pinky's voice was calm and measured.

"We're here, Pinky!" Marta said for me.

"You're right on course from what I can see. Good job."

Outside, the flames had faded, and above the flattening horizon, the dark sky was just beginning to show the first signs of blue. The hand-shaped continent was dead ahead and clearer now, the high ridges of the first "finger" of land broadside to us and growing. Beyond was the second finger and past that, our ultimate destination, a rumpled landscape in mottled gray and green.

Landing was a lot easier than re-entry. I took a chance on the auto-compensators, ready to cut them off if the gig started flailing around, but the forward jets worked in perfect tandem with the ventrals, killing our forward velocity. We settled onto a big flat field, a set of landing stalks extruding at the last minute. I couldn't have done it better myself.

In fact, in hindsight, I wasn't sure I could have done it at all by myself. Antigrav landings were one thing; powered thrust landings, especially complicated ones like this one, were something else. I shivered. I needed to stop jumping into things with half-plans. Then I remembered why I was down here in the first place. Half-plans were all that time afforded.

Marta unstrapped and got to her feet. She bounced experimentally. "I feel light. Definitely lower gee. It's nice." She leaned over to unstrap me. I brushed her hands away.

"I got it," I said testily. At her crestfallen expression, I quickly added, "Sorry. Got the flight jitters."

She gave me a half-hearted smile. "It's okay. I know you don't like being mothered."

I shook my head. "No excuse for being rude. Really, I'm sorry." I looked at her until her face softened into a real smile. Then I reached for the shuttle's bay controls. "Anyway, we're not going anywhere, so I don't need to unstrap," I said. "I'm going to open the cargo hold, fill it with air, and you can run tests on it on the way back?"

"I was planning on getting some specimens," she said. "There's life here. It's probably a good idea to at least take a quick sample."

"The sooner we're up, the more lives we can save," I pointed out.

"I'll make it quick. It's not just a matter of bringing air up. With the *Émilie* in the shape it's in, we're going to need to bring people *down* almost as fast. I want to make sure the ground cover isn't instantly toxic or something."

She was already cycling the bridge lock. Nothing stopped her when she'd set her mind to something. I unsnapped and followed her through. The bay lock wouldn't open until the bridge lock was closed. It was a tiny space, barely big enough for both of us to squeeze in side by side, Marta punched the inner portal closed and reached for the outer lock controls. She paused and looked at me. "I liked your dress, by the way."

"My… oh, right." Lord, I'd forgotten all about it. The special dress I'd made for Jumping Out. The one I'd gotten to wear maybe a couple of hours before swapping it for simpler clothes that would fit under a pressure suit for when we revived Unger. "Thanks for noticing."

"Of course I noticed," she said with a little giggle. Then she cycled the outer lock, and an alien world's light streamed in.

It took a moment for my eyes to adjust. It was brilliant out there, a brightness I hadn't experienced since Hyvilma. The colors were vivid: green to the distant horizon uninterrupted by peaks. A cyan brighter and richer than that on Pureté marked the cloudless dome of the sky. We made our way down the steps and tread gingerly on the ground cover. It wasn't grass or clover, but something in between with leaves shaped like… I couldn't remember the name, something from math class. At first, I thought the whole plain was nothing but these plants, but as I looked around, I made out clumps of something bigger, like thin intertwined trunks each topped with a drooping parasol of waxy green. Those big flat leaves stirred with a breeze which, glancing at my readouts, I saw blew air that was a balmy 285° K.

"I'm not a planetologist," I said, "but this all looks pretty good."

Marta had already gotten two sample bottles of air and was squatting over the dirt, pulling at a plant with a tool. It popped out of the ground fairly easily, trailing a frizzy set of pale roots. The ground wasn't moist, but it wasn't too dry, either.

"Mmm hmm," she said. "Definitely carbon-based with some kind of chlorophyll analog." She kept talking as she pulled another sample. "Those cardioid leaves remind me of Tussilago, but the regularity is really interesting, the way they make almost perfect circles around the stem."

I snapped my fingers, though the effect was lost with the gloves on. "Cardioid. That's the word I was looking for."

"It looks like the dominant ground cover here. I don't see… oh here's another kind." She pulled up another sample and put it in a pouch. "That's probably enough of that for now."

"Anything moving? Critters?"

"Not that I can see. Let me get a couple of scoops of earth to take back and we can go."

Marta grabbed a little sphere off of the belt around her close-fitted suit. She laid it on the ground, tapped it, and it grew into a hand-sized bowl, which she used like a shovel until it was full. Another tap, and the hemisphere sealed itself. She handed it to me without looking and took another sample. Then she straightened out and made a quick survey from left to right, taking in the whole of the new vista.

"There'll be a lot to look at when we come back down," she said wistfully, "but that's for later." She looked down at the bottles of alien air. They had a little display of lights I couldn't interpret. "I'm not reading any obvious toxins. Let's go fill up the bay."

I nodded, hopped back up the stairs to cycle the outer lock. I had to override the safety to get the inner lock to open. There was a big rush of wind as the unpressurized bay filled with alien air. Marta had just enough time to get a third sample.

We fairly sprinted to the cockpit after sealing the bay. I took a seat and drew in a deep breath. The bottled air remained as sterile and tasteless as always. For a moment, I thought about doffing my helmet. The cabin had maintained pressure, after all. No, better safe than sorry. Besides, it wasn't as if the shuttle's air supply would be any more fresh.

The power plant was still warm. Green lights popped up across the panel as I ran the preflight checks again. I saw no reason to delay. I snapped the harness over me, then looked over at Marta to make sure she was also strapped in. She was, hands gripping the chair rests. Another deep breath. This would be my first ride from ground to orbit on thrust rather than antigrav. Could I handle it?

Did I have a choice? I triggered the liftoff jets.

The ground effect nozzles sprayed exhaust, pushing us slowly into the air in a mirror of our landing. The vista spread, the horizon creeping further away, and the tips of faraway mountains came into view. At around 500 meters, I angled the jets, tilting the ship until we were lying on our backs.

"Hang on to your heels," I said, and hit the main rockets.

The automatic limiters kept the gees from piling on too quickly. Still, we hit two gees in seconds, and we were edging toward three after half a minute. Fuel wasn't a problem; I could have gone as high as seven gees if I wanted, and we were in a hurry. But Marta started gasping at three and a half, and I wasn't enjoying it either. I throttled back to three and threw Pinky's return course onto the Window, keeping us on path.

It was finally sinking in: I was riding a rocket into space! I was on top of an arrow of flame headed for the stars like Tereshkova and Özatay nearly a thousand years ago. I felt my smile broaden, though it must have looked like a grimace, the pressure of acceleration pressing my lips back. This is how I'd always imagined space travel, even though twenty years of gentle antigravity ascents should have taught me differently. There were even exciting shudders as we crashed through successive layers of the atmosphere, jiggling my voice as I called out our altitude so Pinky and whomever else was listening in back on the *Émilie* could keep track of our progress.

The shuddering became a bucking, and things stopped being so fun. Yellow lights flickered on, and the exhaust chamber pressure showed high. Had I pushed beyond the tolerance limits of the shuttle? Or was there damage that hadn't made itself apparent until now? I didn't want to reduce thrust, not when every minute mattered. A loud *spang* and an orange flicker changed my mind in a hurry. I cut acceleration to two gees and things smoothed out some. Well, we were going plenty fast now; two gees would get us to orbit quickly enough.

In fact, getting to orbit was a much faster deal than landing. Just 15 minutes from launch, our trajectory was nearly parallel to the ground, and we were right on the invisible highway Pinky's plot guided me to. I switched off the engines, and the abrupt return to weightlessness whipped my ponytail forward in my helmet past my left cheek.

Marta let out her breath in a whoosh, then laughed weakly. "So much for doing analysis on the way up!"

I waved at the Window, the navigation display a glowing set of lines inset against the black sky and lighted horizon of the planet. I grunted in dismay, seeing the time estimated to reach the *Émilie*. "It'll be a bit before we can dock," I said, looking over at the tube she was detaching from her belt. "What can you do without your lab?"

She inspected the specimen, then tapped at her *sayar* with her free hand. Displays popped up in front of her. "I can do a lot, actually. Measure the components down to fractions of a percent, identify obvious toxins. I can even see microorganisms."

The tube lit up with a soft blue glow, and one of the displays went bright. I watched, fascinated, as the luminescence resolved to little floating motes. Marta directed the zoom and focus with deft fingertips. A ragged brown flake, five centimeters across in the display, tumbled lazily in the view. It blurred, disappeared, and was replaced by a coiled strand, like a bit of rope. The view zoomed in further, and now we were looking at little discs floating around, bumping into each other. They had the fuzzy look of things viewed at high magnification.

"Bacteria, or something like it," Marta explained.

"That's bad, right?"

"Well, it's expected. There's a complicated ecology down there. Anyway, even most Terran bacteria are benign. Alien stuff is probably more so."

"You don't sound certain."

She shrugged. "I won't know until I can grow it in tissue analogs. But statistically, we should be alright."

Statistics. A fancy way of saying odds. And no matter what the odds said was likely to happen, somehow I kept running into the most improbable situations. I thought about saying as much, but she'd gone silent, the little furrow between her eyebrows appearing as she worked.

Instead, I slumped back into my chair and watched the counter showing the distance between us and the *Émilie* shrink.

Chapter 13

We left the gig in standby mode after we got back. As soon as Marta got the air checked out, it'd be ready for another run. After leaving Marta in the wardroom, I went straight to the bridge, got in my couch, and had the Window feed the views from everyone's holos as well as a map showing their positions based on their transponders. Only Fareedh was onboard *Majera*. He'd taken over for Pinky on the bridge. Sirena, Unger, and Pinky were clustered on Deck 13. Looming in Sirena's view was a cryobed, already brightly lit with the revival sequence. The person inside had short dark hair floating around her broad face, eyes still closed. Pinky's glowing position dot showed that he was moving methodically around the edge of the pressurized area of the deck. It didn't look like his prior ritualistic pattern, more like he was making sure the seals on his makeshift compartment were secure.

Peter was much deeper in the ship, clumping on magnesticky boots from console to burned out console among the corpses on Deck 11. I closed my eyes and shuddered. I had to give him credit. I don't think I could have been in there among all the death and ruin.

"He's been at it for the last hour," Fareedh said. I swiveled to face him. He had a half dozen displays called up, most of them filled with letter salads that meant nothing to me.

"What's he doing?"

"After he and Pinky finished the seal on 13, he went down to check the main linkages. Good news: he said the power plant and the antigravity are in better shape than he thought. Not that there's any need to risk turning it on. He's checking on the Drive compartment now."

"Are the others reviving a shuttle pilot?"

He stretched his long arms as if he'd been in a cramped position for a while. "Shari Chang. Some kind of flight engineer. Unger picked her almost immediately, so she must be the best for the job."

"How about you? Figured out how to stop the awakenings?"

His eyebrow quirked. "The *Émilie's* ship's *sayar* is a mess. There're at least three subsystems responsible for the breakdown. You know you're asking for a miracle, right?"

I smiled bleakly. "Got any for me?"

He snorted a chuckle, the smile remaining on his face. "As a matter of fact..."

"Wait. Really?!"

"Here's what I can do." His fingers glided over his panel, and one of the displays glowed with a blue border. It was more gibberish. He paused, looking at me intensely. "We're actually very lucky. I know we blame ourselves for this mess, and maybe we're the proximate cause, but we also very well could have come across a dark ship. It's that bad."

The shivers returned. "You said something about a miracle?"

He nodded. "I'm not sure why the revival sequences triggered on all decks. It's not an emergency protocol. I think it was triggered from Deck 11, some sort of short in the revival system. Normally, the crew would choose who to revive and when, not bring them all out. But the program modules are all so much Gruyère. A lot of systems are running through auxiliary modules, back ups with less functionality. We're lucky everything's so redundant. I can't stop the awakenings because the routine that handles the command to start the revival sequences is pretty much gone." He pointed out a section of code that wasn't even nonsense programming words but actual garbage characters. "But there's one routine over here I kept seeing called from lots of different modules." The display blurred, went to more code salad. "I didn't want to fiddle with it much because I don't know what'll happen. But this thing here is clearly the counter..."

"So you reset the counter," I cut in.

He laughed through his nose. "No. I can't see the actual numbers."

"Get to the point, Fareedh!"

"I can change the *base* the numbers are measured in. There are a few options. Base-16 is the highest it'll let me choose, so I changed it to that."

I tried to remember my bases. I knew binary was ones and zeroes. Base-16 was bigger than the usual Base-10. "So you got, what, 60% more time?"

"Bases are exponential. We've got a little more than three days."

"Three days! That changes everything!" Time enough for more than a dozen flights. Plenty of time to get air onto every deck, especially if I had help.

He smiled. "Maybe. If the air you brought back checks out, and if Chang can fly the other shuttle, and if we can make sure the hull is airtight..."

"Then we just might make it."

His smile broadened, white teeth shining. "We just might."

I leaned forward and clasped his hands. "Thank you, Fareedh. You've saved everyone."

Fareedh's cheeks got a lot redder than I thought they could, and he blinked in a nervous, completely un-Fareedh-like way. "I try," he stammered.

I felt myself blushing too, letting his hands go and turning my gaze to the Window.

"Sorry," I said. "Habit."

"I don't mind," he said lightly.

I bit my lip. I should have been elated, but instead, I was suddenly feeling very nervous. I guess it made sense. With the weight of ten thousand lives lifted, all the other issues I'd been dealing with clamored for attention. There was one that needed resolution right away.

"No," I said at last. "It's not fair to you."

There was a pause. The air circulator came on and thrummed for a moment, then went off.

Fareedh said, "I take it you made a decision?"

I looked up at him, trying to smile. "Not exactly?" The smile faded. "No, that's not fair either." I took a deep breath, which caught rather than coming out in words. What did I want to say?

His expression softened. "You're just not feeling it."

I wanted to tell him that wasn't the case. That he was handsome and wonderful and I loved him, and it was just a bad time.

My lips, on the other hand, simply blurted out, "Yeah."

A brief flash of disappointment crossed his features, quickly extinguished, replaced by a sad smile. "It's okay. It really is." He looked away, drummed his fingers on his panel a couple of times. Then he thumbed his *sayar*, the displays collapsing into the device. "I'll, uh, keep working on this in my quarters. I'll let you know if I find anything new."

Fareedh left, and I crossed my arms to grip my shoulders, feeling like a Grade A jerk. Then I shook my head, took a deep breath, and commed Marta to tell her that Fareedh had bought us more time.

Not too much later, Sirena let me know Chang's revival was done. I thought about suiting up to join them, but I was the lone person watching the displays. In any event, Chang was going to eventually end up here anyway. Instead, I checked up on Peter.

"Kitra, you've got to see this," he was saying, turning so his view focused on a dimly glowing section of… something.

"You're on Level 2?" I asked, noting his position dot.

"Mmmm. I mean, yes. This *was* the Drive deck." His tone was disbelieving.

"What am I looking at? It seems like some kind of fluorescent sheet holo or something. Like something they'd project on the walls of *Le Frontiére* on a dance night."

Big, suited hands reached out in the display, gripping a *sayar*. After a moment, Peter said, "It's a kind of residue. This whole deck is glowing with some kind of radiation."

I cleared a dry throat. "Should you maybe not be in there?"

"I don't think it's dangerous. It's not registering on most of my meters. I'm surprised I can see it at all, actually. The wavelengths are too short. This must be secondary interference." He sounded puzzled. "No, that can't be. There's no air for it to interact with."

Beyond the ghostly lavender sheen, the wide expanse of the deck seemed strangely empty, with only the vague suggestion of equipment against the far wall. The room was huge and should have been crowded with Drive machinery, an assembly big enough to take a massive ship like the *Émilie* and send it a dozen light years at a time through space.

"Peter, where's the Drive?"

"You noticed, huh? I'm betting it stayed in hyperspace. That may be where all the air went, too. Watch."

I heard a faint hiss over the comms. A pink fog billowed in the display. It looked like the distress aerosol we carried on our suit belts. The mist slowly oozed into a tightening spiral toward the center of the flat glow. Then it was gone. I lurched forward in my chair.

"Peter, there's a crack in the universe right in front of you."

"Where did the spray go?!"
"Yeah, that's a good question, isn't it?"

I was suddenly very cold. It was like the *Émilie* had never quite gotten out of Jump. It was still connected to hyperspace somehow.

"Peter, there's a crack in the universe right in front of you. Maybe you shouldn't be standing so close."

He let out a strangled laugh. "You're probably right. Kitra, there's something very odd going on here." The glow faded in his view as he backed away, toward the central axis of the colony ship.

"Well, luckily we won't have to stay here for long," I said. "Fareedh says he's bought us enough time to pump in air, revive the refugees, and get them down to the surface."

His sigh of relief was a loud crackle over the comms.

"D'you tell the others?"

"Yeah." I made a quick mental checklist. Marta had been first, then Pinky, then Sirena, who'd told Unger. That was everyone.

"Always the last to know," he mock-grumbled.

"You mean saving the best for last," I corrected. "So this hyperspace crack is the reason *Émilie*'s air tanks are empty?" I asked.

"Sort of," he replied. He was swinging open the axis hatch and clambering out. He was very careful not to float, keeping his magnetized soles on a solid surface at all times. "The tanks are on Decks 3 and 4 along with other ship's stores. What I got out of the logs is that they triggered open when the ship came out of Jump, and all of the air eventually leaked through the Drive section. At least, I hope that's what happened. If the hull is cracked, it'll be hard to fill it with air."

"What'll you do about Level 2?"

"We can seal that off more easily than we can seal the whole ship. Anyway, we just need to air-proof the sleeper levels. We can do that one at a time if we have to."

There was a tap on the jamb of the bridge door. I turned to see Sirena glide her chair into the cabin with a woman with chin-length dark hair—Chang, I realized—behind her. The engineer was wearing an unfitted suit, one of our spares. Or it could have been from the *Émilie*, but ship's gig aside, I figured we were relying on the colony ship's gear as little as possible.

Chang's face had the puffy look of the just-awakened, but I pegged her at middle age, anywhere from 40 to 80. Despite her bleariness, she managed a smile and even a little bow. She was almost as short as me.

"You're Captain Yilmaz?" she asked. Her high voice was hoarse with the remnants of cold sleep.

"I'm Kitra," I said.

"Ah. Then I'm Shari," she said with a tired grin. The accent was on the 'Sha'.

I gestured to Peter's empty seat. "If I'd known you were coming so soon, I'd have dropped the gravity to make it easier for you."

She waved a hand dismissively. "I've been lying down a long time, longer than expected, so they tell me. It's nice to be up. The doc says you took one of the gigs down to the surface?"

I exchanged glances with Sirena. She looked amused. "I like 'doc' better than 'Your Highness'." Shari looked quizzically at her, but she pretended not to notice.

"I did take the gig down. We got a load of air. Marta—you haven't met her yet, she's the life system's expert—she's checking it out for issues."

Shari nodded, a stubby fingered hand on her hip. "How did it fly?"

"Well, we made it back. It got rough on the way, though. Hopefully not anything serious."

"I'll give both of the gigs a good going over," she said.

I looked down at the deck. "I'm sorry about all this. I know you didn't expect your trip to end this way." I looked back up at her round face.

Her dark eyes crinkled sympathetically at the edges. "At least we made the trip. From what I understand, we're amazingly fortunate. I know some of us lost the lottery, but given the odds we were facing if we stayed on Gloire, I'd call your being here a miracle." She pronounced the final word with a certain reverence. The effect was undercut by a loud, liquidy growl that came from her midsection. The engineer gripped her belly and grinned. "And after a quick trip to the galley, I'll get right to work on those shuttles."

I laughed, giving my best rendition of a salute. It seemed appropriate. She nodded and disappeared into the wardroom.

"What are you going to do now?" I asked Sirena.

She blew out her breath, shaking her head with a jingle of earrings. "While I've still got some of Fareedh's potent tea percolating in me, I think I'm going to revive the next patient. I suggested a doctor be the next one to awaken, and Their Grace, the Minister, has made a selection."

It dawned on me that Sirena looked older now, somehow, her features drawn and pale. Seeing her fatigue made me realize that I was flagging a bit, too. I stifled a yawn, wondering if I had time to make a real cup of coffee.

The princess flashed a smile at me. "You should take a proper nap, darling. If you're really going to be flying air in with Shari over the next few days, you'll want to be rested." She added with a wink, "Doctor's orders." Then she was through the door, too. I stretched hard, feeling vertebrae crack, and ended up on my feet. I needed to do a better job with my posture. All the slouching in seats all day was going to give me a permanent hunch. I leaned over to tap the panel.

"Hey, Pinky," I called out.

He answered immediately, "That's me."

"Where are you?" I didn't see his dot on the *Émilie* diagram.

"In which coordinate system would you like the answer?"

I snorted. "Show off. Are you busy, or can you come spell me on the bridge?"

"I'm just de-suiting now. I'll be happy to come up once I've finished letting it all hang out."

"Thank you for the image. I'll be here."

I stretched again and this time let my yawn out without restraint. I felt a little bad about abandoning my post. That brought an old memory floating back to me, a conversation I'd had with Erkki. He was the wrinkled owner of *Le Frontiére*, the coffee shop that had practically been our second home before *Majera* took that role. In the midst of one of the old skipper freighter's anecdotes was a snatch of wisdom that had always stuck in my mind: "Rest is a pilot's duty, too."

I smiled as I got up. Sometimes it just takes someone else giving you permission to relax.

Chapter 14

Consciousness returned gradually. Over time, it came to me that the flat cream void in front of my eyes was the wall a half-meter away. I took that deep intake of breath that always accompanies waking and rolled onto my back, blinking. The uninterrupted nap had left me clear-headed and relaxed. I stretched, keeping my back flat to the bed. It was nice, not feeling any pressure, any responsibility, just laying there. There was a turmoil just under the surface; I knew it would come flooding through given the chance. I just focused on the now, letting the worries stay in the back of my mind.

Rolling onto my left side, my eyes flickered over the souvenir table. *I should have picked something up from the planet*, was my first thought, immediately followed by the memory that I'd be going back down soon enough. And *that* was followed by remembering that I'd be going down to the surface at least a half-dozen times over the next couple of days. The dam burst. All the stressors and concerns came to the fore, and I was wide awake.

I called out to my *sayar* to reach Marta. She answered almost immediately, her face popping up a foot above where I'd carelessly dropped the device on the floor.

"You're up," she said cheerfully.

"Looks like it," I said, rubbing my eyes. They were gritty. "How long was I out?"

"Just a couple of hours. I have good news."

I sat up and yawned, not bothering to cover my mouth.

"Don't look so excited," she giggled.

"Sorry."

"That's all right. I've run the air samples from the planet through a full analysis." Her eyes gleamed. "No toxins, a reasonable partial pressure of carbon dioxide, plenty of oxygen. Maybe a little overmuch. It'll be stimulating."

"No bugs then?"

"Oh, plenty of bugs," she said with a toss of her curls. "But I can't get them to do much with my tissue samples. I'd say they're harmless, at least in the short term."

"Good enough," I said. "We've got enough problems in the short term. So, I guess the next step is to get some air to fill the decks?"

Peter's face sprang into existence next to Marta's, the display growing to accommodate them both. They were in the same room. "It'll take two loads per deck. In any event, first we'll want to make sure the *Émilie* is airtight so we don't have the problem you saw on Level 2. We won't need to go anywhere near full pressure for that, so I can get started right away."

This time I stifled the yawn, then wrinkled my nose. My breath was terrible. And I had to pee.

"Let's have a quick conference before we all go out again. Give me five minutes to freshen up?"

Peter nodded. "Sure. I'll tell the others. See you soon."

Sirena and Unger were on Deck 13 reviving someone, and Shari was looking over the gig I'd taken out, so it was just Peter, Marta, Fareedh and Pinky in the wardroom. As I took my seat, I had a moment of déjà vu. We were back in the Jump from Jaiyk to Vatan, at maximum range and wondering if the capacitors Peter had kluged into our system would have enough power to get us home.

This time was different, of course. On the one hand, now it wasn't us who needed saving; it was ten thousand sleeping souls. On the other hand, we had a good plan to get everyone revived and out of danger, one that felt a lot more certain of success than that last wild ride home had been.

I yawned yet again, and Fareedh said, "I've got just the thing." If I'd been more awake, I'd have read more meaning into the glances Peter and Marta exchanged. Instead, I accepted the steaming mug of tea that Fareedh offered me, remembering the comforting spiciness of the brew I'd had last time I visited his quarters.

The first sip made my lips purse and my eyes water. It was beyond bitter, like eating the side of a tree. Fareedh must have forgotten to dilute it. I got it down, but it took an effort of will to swallow. To my credit, I did *not* cough.

"What is this, Fareedh? Pure *zavarka*? You're supposed to add water!" I wondered if it was some kind of practical joke.

He did not quite manage to suppress an evil grin. "Not exactly *zavarka*. It'll wake you up nicely, though."

"This must be what you gave Sirena," I said weakly with a constricted throat. I noticed now just how dark the liquid in the cup was.

Fareedh nodded. "She's had three cups today so far. I can get you something to sweeten it if you like."

I gave him a withering look and then made a show of draining the cup. It was scalding hot, at least, and when it was done, my heart was pounding. I wiped off my lips with the back of my hand and said, "I always did want more hair on my chest. Thanks, Fareedh."

"No problem," he said with a wiggle of his eyebrows. "That's how I got mine."

Pinky stretched a pseudopod across the table toward the pot at Fareedh's elbow. "Let me try that stuff," he said.

Peter swatted it in mid-grab. "Can we get on with things, please?" The long, pink arm quickly retracted. Peter nodded and pushed tousled blond hair out his eyes. "Here's what I've got. I've got my *sayar* hooked into the pressure sensors on every deck of the Émilie. I've also planted portable ones of my own, some along the axis of the ship, the rest on the sleeper decks. Anything above a millibar of pressure will trigger them."

"Do you need to run a hose or something to the decks?" I asked.

"Nah. We just open the axis door and the deck hatches, then open the gig's hold."

"That's it? Isn't the ship too big for that?"

"Gas quickly expands to equally fill a space," Pinky said. "Would you like me to demonstrate?"

"No!" Marta and I cried in unison.

"Just trying to help…"

I ignored him, "How long until Sirena revives the next patient?"

"She already has," Marta answered. "Or at least, she's confirmed things are going according to plan. She's actually doing two at a time. When Fareedh's timer runs down, we're going to need as many people tending the sleepers' recovery as possible."

"That's great news. Is there anything else?"

Fareedh leaned back in his chair. "I've been going over the subsystems in the *Émilie*'s ship's *sayar*. Not touching anything, mind you. Just seeing how everything fits together and determining what parts aren't working properly. It's all pretty standard stuff I've seen before, except for the advanced drive code, which I didn't bother with. I was able to see where routines had clearly gotten mangled. There are some redundant systems we could patch in as required, and I could also program working routines onto undamaged memory sections."

"What for?" I asked. "We're abandoning this ship as soon as we can, aren't we?"

He shrugged. "A lot can go wrong in three days. I want to be able to act in a flash if needed."

"Sounds like you figured out a lot while I was asleep."

Fareedh glanced over to his left at Peter. "I had help." Peter's lips quirked into a smile. It seemed I was missing context.

But there was stuff to do, and I felt Fareedh's tea kicking in. I pushed my chair out and stood. "Speaking of acting in a flash, I'd better go lend a hand to Shari. The sooner we start hauling air, the better."

"No one's hauling air," came the voice from the door. I whipped my head around to see Shari, suit smudged and dark eyes hooded. "Those gigs can't re-enter."

"What are you talking about?" I demanded.

"You and her," the engineer said, nodding to Marta, "were awfully lucky. Your issue started about 100 kilometers up?"

"That sounds right."

"I went through the logs. You had exhaust regulators fail in three of the seven ports. If you hadn't dropped thrust when you did, the thing would have blown apart."

I nodded slowly, feeling the chill return.

"We can't use that gig again without a full servicing," she continued.

"But we did make it back. Couldn't we just take it easy?"

She shook her head. "I wouldn't take that chance. You could maybe use the thrusters for close orbital maneuvers. It's airtight at least. You might even get it down to the planet again, once. But coming back?" Her hair fluttered as she shook her head again.

"Well, we've got the other gig at least," Peter said. Then added more faintly, "Don't we?"

"I can't even get that one to power up. Not even using an external *sayar* patch. There's some kind of burn that goes through the circuitry, like it got slashed with a laser. Something like that might have happened with the other one, too. They were brand new when we got them. Yours shouldn't have failed."

"Both shuttles," I said, my voice trembling. "They're both broken."

Mouth set in a hard grimace, Shari's eyes met mine. She didn't say any more. She didn't have to.

Without the shuttles, there was no way to get air in the ship. Without air, even with the extra time Fareedh had bought us, the people of Gloire were still doomed.

Cramps hit my stomach. I felt like I was going to throw up. No, I *was* going to throw up. I fluttered my hands a moment, managed an "Excuse me a sec," and punched the door to my cabin.

My throat felt like fire, and the taste was the sour flavor of Fareedh's tea. My breath came out in ragged bursts. I caught a glimpse of myself in the mirror above the sink and recoiled at the sight. For a moment, my blotched face was actually a welcome distraction. Then the magnitude of the situation hit me again. Luckily, there was no more lunch to lose.

We were right back where we started. Except this time, I'd gotten hopeful that we could save *all* of the people from Gloire. Before, I could count even a few lives saved as a win. Now, the ones we could revive with the air we had felt like nothing compared to the numbers that were going to die.

There was a well of tears inside me ready to burst. I wanted to sob. I wanted to scream.

I did neither.

I splashed some water on my face, waited for the worst of the blotchiness to go down, and cycled the disposal. On my way out, almost as an afterthought, I popped a refresher in my mouth, feeling the tingly aroma-canceller do its work. Then I opened the door.

Eyes flicked up to mine as I walked in. They hadn't been speaking to each other; they must have been stunned by the news, my abrupt departure, or both.

"Sorry about that," I managed. "Probably Fareedh's killer brew." I gripped the back of my chair, not wanting to sit down. "So, we're going to Plan B," I said.

Peter looked at me wearily. "What's Plan B?"

I shook my head sadly. "I don't know."

Silence again.

"Could we use your ship?" Shari asked. "It's not damaged."

"I could take *Majera* down, but our hold carries a bare fraction of what the gigs do," I said.

Peter amplified me. "At best, we could maybe fill a deck in time."

"It's something," Fareedh said.

"Can you buy us more time?" I asked him.

He clicked his tongue in the negative. "I've used up my tricks. The system managing the cryobeds is one of the worst damaged. If I play around with it, anything could happen." His low voice was bleak, defeated.

I turned to Shari. "You said one of the gigs *could* land. I could shuttle air up while you put a load of your people on the gig to revive on the surface." I tried doing the math in my head to see how many sleepers we could fit in the bay of a shuttle. It was like trying to spread cold butter. Two thirds of my brain was shut down.

"It won't work," Marta said. "You'd have to remove the beds from *Émilie's* power system. They'd all start reviving as soon as we got out of the hangar."

I bit my lip, and my fingers started rubbing each other.

There was a gentle pressure on my shoulder. Pinky had stretched out a big, three-fingered hand. At first I thought he was trying to comfort me. Then I saw the shocking orange of his skin, the nervous rippling beneath.

"Kitra," he said in a voice that didn't sound human at all, made of a thousand spikes and devoid of inflection. "Kitra, we've got to save them. If we don't, they'll have nowhere to go. No one to remember them."

The *alienness* of the voice shocked me. I'd never heard him talk like that before. I'd never seen him this color either. He must have been terrified. I gripped his hand, warm and rubbery. It was trembling.

"I don't know what to do," I said.

The whorls of his eyespots met my eyes. "Please." The sound was ragged, heart wrenching.

I wanted to scream at him. There was no way to get air up to the ship! We were helpless up here. Lord, the irony of it all. All that air was just a few hundred kilometers away and we couldn't reach any of it. And the *Émilie* wasn't built for landing without a pad.

Hang on a minute.

"Peter," I said.

He jolted slightly. "What?"

"The power plant on the *Émilie*. Fareedh says you checked it over and it works, right?"

"Ye-es."

"How well?"

He shrugged. "It's a tough system, and it's far from the Drive deck. It managed to keep the cryobeds going this whole time. I don't know that I'd want to push it..."

"What about the antigravity?" I cut in.

"The thrusters, maybe. All the internals above Deck 1 are out."

Shari asked sharply, "What are you thinking?"

"It's like the proverb: If we can't bring air to the *Émilie*, we need to bring *Émilie* to the air." I paused, then, "We've got to land it."

There was chaos for a moment.

"You can't..."

"There's no way..."

"...burn up..."

Shari motioned for silence and, amazingly, got it. "This ship isn't designed for atmospheric entry."

"That was my first thought. But it's airtight, isn't it? It can take the stress of Jump. If we can land, we can bring in all the air we want in an instant."

"The bottom's not flat," Fareedh noted.

"It's flat-*ish*," I said.

"It'll ruin the ship," Shari objected. "We'll be stuck on the planet."

"It's not like you were going anywhere in the *Émilie* anyway."

"Great infinity," Peter said. "We're going 40,000 kilometers an hour. We'd have to lose all of that velocity, and then descend slowly enough to not burn up."

"And not crash," Marta added, but there was hope in her voice.

"Right. All those things. Peter, can we do it?" I asked.

Peter looked at Shari, then at Fareedh. "I wouldn't want to get your hopes up. With our luck, the whole system could go ZZORT!" He threw his hands up to accent the gesture.

"That's where we are anyway," I said.

"That's not true," Shari pointed out. "If we don't touch anything, we can probably save a few hundred. If the system shorts out or we crash, we lose everyone."

She was right. It was a gamble.

"I think it's worth a shot," I said.

Silence. At last, Marta spoke up, her voice serene, penetrating as a bell. "This didn't happen by chance, our coming here. Everything's connected. If we weren't supposed to save the refugees, we never would have picked this planet or come when we did." She looked at Peter, who looked back for a moment, then nodded in agreement.

Pinky's orange had mellowed to a faint ochre. When he spoke, his voice had regained some texture, though it still had a flat aspect. "You are all so alone," he said to Shari. "A few dozen cannot preserve the whole. We must try."

"He's right," came Unger's voice through the comms. I hadn't realized they'd been open. Maybe Pinky had done it. "Gloire cannot survive as a fragment of itself. While we all live, we must try to save us all."

I looked at Pinky for a silent moment, not certain he and the minister had meant quite the same thing. It didn't matter, though. We had made a decision.

"Then we do everything we can in the next three days to make it work," I said, determination pushing aside uncertainty. "We get this ship patched so it can land, and we take her down."

Peter unfolded his arms, expression no less doubtful. Then his features cleared, and he nodded.

I looked up at the ceiling, toward the deity my mom had prayed to, whose existence I'd never felt certain of, even when I went through the motions of devotion.

I sure hope you're listening. We need all the help we can get.

The first thing we did was send a drone outside the *Émilie* to get another look at its rear end. It wasn't *so* bad. No apparent damage, and while the engine end of the ship wasn't entirely flat, it was symmetrical. If we managed to get the refugee ship down in one piece, it could settle on its hind end and stay upright. Even landing slightly off kilter would be okay; so long as the antigravity thrusters worked, we could straighten out the ship after it landed. And if the thrusters failed *before* landing, well, the *Émilie* would crash and that would be that.

The next thing to do was the really important one. We had to make sure the *Émilie*'s hull was sound. According to Peter, when the Drive had imploded, or gotten sucked away, it had caused some kind of intangible energy surge, mostly moving forward through the control linkages along the inner edge of the *Émilie*'s hull and converging on Deck 11: the flight deck. That, in turn, had caused a more conventional explosion on the flight deck, sending shrapnel and focused radiation forward in a star pattern. That's why as we went down the ship's levels toward Deck 11, the power grid and the sleepers who'd been attached to it had been more strongly affected.

Neither the surge nor either of the explosions had pierced the three armored decks that contained hydrogen so compressed it was a liquid. If that had happened, well, there wouldn't have been an *Émilie* to find; the volatile hydrogen would have exploded in a rush.

That didn't mean the outer hull hadn't been breached, though. The good news was that the power grid was uninterrupted along the colony ship's outer walls, but even hairline cracks could be fatal under the stress of reentry. Especially with the internal antigravity mostly out. Without that stabilizing bubble along the ship, every shudder and strain was going to go directly into the hull without shock absorption. Hundreds of thousands of tons, all precariously balanced on their end, could easily break into pieces.

So we had to look for leaks. Luckily, we had that gig's hold worth of air. We'd originally planned to use it to make sure the *Émilie* was airtight so we could pressurize the ship. Now we were doing the opposite, looking for holes that would compromise our ability to land.

Come test time, Shari was on the gig. Peter was on Deck 1. Up on the Window, I had a big display of all the pressure sensors he'd planted along the ship. They made a skeletal outline of the *Émilie*, composed of black dots against a gray background.

I licked my lips. "Are you ready to vent?" I commed.

The flight engineer's voice came through as clearly as if she was in the same room. "Any time."

"Just half of the load," Unger's voice cut in. "We'll want a reserve for selected revivals."

Shari: "You got it, boss."

I waited for any further objections. There weren't any. "Let's do it," I said.

Almost immediately the black dots representing the hangar deck burst into color, progressing from deep red to a bright orange as air spread through the chamber. The rest of *Émilie's* sensors stayed dark; we'd closed the axis hatch for the first test. I tapped the panel and numbers appeared beside the dots. 10.234 kilopascals, less than a tenth standard pressure. Seconds went by. The orange lights remained perfectly steady, the air pressure readouts not changing to the limit of their accuracy.

"Hangar deck is airtight," I said in an exhale of breath. "One down, sixteen to go."

"The others are going to go a lot faster," Fareedh noted.

"That's true," I said. "Peter, have you got all the axis doors open?"

"All except Level 2," came the reply. "We're just going to have to hope on that one."

I shook my head. That was the looniest thing about the plan. Not only would we not know if there were cracks outside the ship on Level 2, but we'd already confirmed there was a crack *inside* the ship on that deck. Who knew what that would mean come re-entry?

At least we could minimize the unknowns. "Pinky?"

"Kitra?" He was a star shape near the hangar's axis hatch, four points anchored to the floor.

"Open it up."

"Aye, Cap'n." His fifth appendage triggered the hatch release, and the portal irised open.

Pinky braced himself against the momentary rush of wind. Sensor lights flickered redly to life along the axis of the ship and in rapid succession from Decks 16 down to 1 as the air filled the Émilie at the speed of sound. The indicator lights settled down and took on the dull color of a fireplace ember.

"I read 603.15 pascals and holding," Peter said. Hardly any pressure at all. If Peter opened his suit, it'd feel the same as if he'd been in raw space. But compared to the vacuum that had filled the colony ship before, the air was infinitely dense.

I checked. The Deck 1 sensors were in almost perfect agreement with the ones scattered throughout the ship. I let out another breath. No leaks.

"That's great," came Peter's voice. "One less thing. I'll get started on the…"

"Wait a minute," Fareedh called. He pointed a long finger at one of the Deck 3 indicators. It read just under 603, and it ticked down a hundredth of a pascal while I watched it. "Peter, can you close the hatch to Deck 3?" he asked.

"Leak?"

"It's something, and we'll start seeing it elsewhere pretty soon if we don't stop it."

"I'm on it."

Peter's position light shifted toward the axis accompanied by muffled footsteps transmitted through his comm. By the time he'd reached Deck 3, the sensors there were down to 602.45, and the sensors along the Émilie's central shaft were also starting to show a drop in pressure. Peter paused at the brink, his display showing a poorly lit chamber through the door crammed with machinery. I couldn't tell if it was cargo or part of the ship, but it looked more like cargo. I heard him gasp.

"What's wrong?" Fareedh asked.

Peter's display didn't move. I lowered the bridge lights to better see what he was seeing. Gradually, I became aware of a dim glow *in* the deck. My breath caught. Purple. The same purple as on Deck 2.

"I… I'm going to have to go in and see what happened." His voice was thin, hesitant. He didn't move.

Seconds passed. I didn't want to push him, considered sending Pinky down instead.

"You want me to suit up and hold your hand?" Fareedh asked.

I expected Peter to ignore the goad or maybe shoot back a snappy reply. Instead, he said, "Maybe when I get back," and with a deep breath clumped into the room. I blinked, looked at Fareedh, who shrugged and smiled enigmatically. Well *that* was new.

"I've got the door closed," Peter commed. "Pressure's still dropping in here. How's it looking out there?"

"Hold on," Fareedh said. "Giving it a second."

The sensors all stayed the same deep red. The pressure drop seemed to have stopped.

"We're good," I called out.

"Yeah," Peter said. "Let me make sure the leak's in the floor, not the hull." He pulled out a seal sheet, the kind used for temporary patching of holes in a ship, expanded it to full size, and gingerly let the thing drop over the center of the purple patch that sprawled over an irregular half square meter on the floor. I half expected the seal to vanish when it touched the glow, but instead, it simply adhered its edges to the deck. The room lost its eerie glow, now lit only by Peter's suit lamps.

"That's better," he said, his tone a little more relaxed.

I felt a warm presence behind me. I turned, looked up into Marta's face. She was watching the display intently. "How's he doing?" she asked.

"Fine," I said. "Just flirting with Fareedh." I'd meant it to come out lightly but didn't quite succeed.

"Again, Peter?" she asked.

"He started it," Peter commed.

I began to say something cute and cutting in reply, swallowed wrong instead, triggering a coughing fit. By the time I was done, Marta was staring at me wide-eyed with concern. I waved my hand to let her know I was okay. As I caught my breath, it dawned on me that Fareedh had just said something.

"What was that?" I asked.

"I said, '*Çok yaşa.*' You sneezed."

147

That made me chuckle. "Oh, *sen de gör.*"

"I'll turn up the humidity when Peter's done," Marta said, eyeing me a moment longer before returning her gaze to the Window.

"I am done," came Peter's voice. "I think I've stopped the leak, which means the outer hull is sound on this level. I can't see the glow anymore either, so it was probably coming from a physical crack in the deck, maybe from when the Drive housing got snapped."

"That's good," Fareedh said. "It means that rift, or whatever it is, is confined to Deck 2."

"I hope so. Anyway, I'm coming out now."

Marta let out a little sigh of relief, and Fareedh shifted in his chair, folding his legs underneath him. I watched as Peter's little position light crept back out into the *Émilie's* central shaft.

"The ship is airtight," I said.

Deck 1 hadn't been built with driving the ship in mind. The *Émilie's* lowest level was mostly for housing the giant fusion engine that powered the colony ship. What comparatively little space there was left over was for access and maintenance. But Deck 1 was where the driving had to be done because Deck 1, aft of the surge, was intact.

After making sure it was airtight, Peter, Fareedh, and Shari worked for eighteen hours setting up a seat-and-console control station. Toward the end, they were relieved by two other engineers Sirena had revived, a twin brother and sister pair who'd been power technicians back on Gloire and had an almost telepathic efficiency. Sirena, Marta, and the revived doctor, I didn't catch his name, had worked almost continuously, waking up as many of the *Glorieux* as they could. By the end of Day 2, the non-sleeping population of the *Émilie* numbered sixteen, including the *Majera* crew.

Day 3 would only have twenty hours, at least only twenty that mattered. If we weren't on the ground by the time the cryobeds opened, it was all over.

Chapter 15

I sat in the Wardroom rubbing my eyes. I'd managed to snatch four hours of sleep despite three cups of coffee and another dose of Fareedh's killer brew. Before I'd gone to bed, I'd helped the twins run the *Émilie's* power plant to 20%, enough to test the ship's internal antigravity. What was left of it worked fine. Next step would be to ensure that the antigrav could project thrust *backward* so that the ship could maneuver and decelerate. If it couldn't, well, we'd saved a measly ten refugees.

Shari came in, her dark hair disheveled. There were sweat stains at the armpits of her gray jumper. She must have just come in from a stint outside. I waved in a friendly manner to the pot of Turkish coffee I'd just brewed — I couldn't take another serving of the stuff the Maker made, even if it was quicker.

"Thanks," she mumbled, taking a spot near me at the end of the table and pouring a cup. She downed it in a gulp without adding sweetener or waiting for it to cool. I respected that.

The silence stretched. To fill it, I said idly, "That pilot station sure is a kludge. Going to be rough flying from there." I hadn't been looking forward to being crammed in a repurposed couch between two walls of machinery, flying a pile of ungainly metal halfway around and then onto a planet, but it was what it was.

She grunted in response. Then she smiled slightly. "Good thing I'm small."

I frowned. "*You're* small?"

"Yeah. Aren't I?"

I snorted slightly. "Well, yeah, but what does that have to do with anything?"

Shari looked confused. "It means I fit the station better than if I were that tree of a programmer you got?"

"That's true, but, why would you be using the station?"

Now she was looking at me like I was speaking English or some other foreign language. "Because I'm landing the *Émilie*?"

"You are? I thought I was!"

That provoked a laugh, a staccato thing like when the Maker tries to fill an order but is out of goop. "Why, by the stars, would you think that?"

I opened my mouth, then shut it.

Shari went on, "Of course I'm flying the *Émilie*." She shook her head. "Sheesh."

I looked down at the table. "I guess I just figured, since we caused all of this, and I'm the pilot..."

She reached out and punched my shoulder lightly. "Hey, kid. Like I said before, we were in all kinds of trouble before you found us. Don't kill yourself over it." The engineer leaned back and poured another cup. "Anyway, you've got to keep to your own ship. Not just to fly escort, but if something goes wrong, to make sure at least some of us make it out."

"That... makes a lot of sense. I should have thought of that."

"Lots to think about lately. Hey, this is really good. I wish I'd let that first cup linger." She waved her mug at me. "Sorry to take so much."

I shook my head. "There's plenty."

"In that case..."

My *sayar* pinged. It was Peter. "What's up?" I asked.

"We're ready to do flight tests whenever you are."

I looked over at Shari. "Should I take the *Majera* out now or wait?"

"I'd wait. The more techies on the ship while we're in orbit, the better. Let's split up when we're getting ready to brake."

"Got it." So much for breakfast. "Let me just Make something portable to eat, and we'll see what the broken beast can do."

I had thought planning the path for the *Émilie* would be the hard part. It wasn't. Even with a messed up ship's *sayar*, plotting courses was no problem. In fact, Fareedh didn't even bother to use the damaged brain of the colony ship. Instead, he programmed a spare personal *sayar* and patched it in. It sounded loony at first, using a tiny device to run such a big ship, but he reminded me that people had been doing orbital maneuvers with spaceships even before they'd invented *sayars*, at least the kind I'm familiar with. I guess they used abacuses or something a thousand years ago.

So the theory was easy. It was the practice we got hung up on.

Shari got the *Émilie*'s plant to 25% and engaged the external maneuvering units. For the first time in half a year, the giant ship started to move. I felt the shuddering right away, a subsonic wave that set my teeth on edge. Out of the corner of my eye, I saw Fareedh fall upon his *sayar* to make adjustments on the fly. Things smoothed out. Outside, through a display that took up most of the Window, the starfield began to shift. After a few seconds, the looming bulk of the planet filled the view. Clouds and sea drifted past in alternating vastness. Then darkness swept that away, and we were looking at stars again.

"Pitch test complete," Shari said from her little cocoon of a station, her face lit from below by her displays.

"No major issues," Fareedh said, though I thought I saw a puzzled look flash across his face.

"Stress is in tolerance range," commed Marie, one of the engineer twins.

"Going for yaw," Shari said.

Once more, stars swung past, perpendicular to paths they'd taken before. The sun briefly flared into view, was dimmed automatically by the Window as it passed, then disappeared out of sight. After a complete pivot, Shari stabilized us. Then she rotated the ship through a full 360 degrees.

"All axes responding," she said at the end of the final test. "Good job, Fareedh."

"I try, *mademoiselle*."

A muffled snort. "Not for decades, kid. All right. I'm going to try an orbit change. Wish me luck."

She might have meant the request rhetorically. There was still a chorus of *bonne chance*, including one from my lips, except I said *bol şanslar* out of habit.

It was not immediately obvious that anything was wrong, but I heard Fareedh tapping again on his device almost instantly. Pinky called out, "We're listing right. There's an imbalance somewhere."

"Should I compensate here or wait for you to fix it?" Shari commed, words clipped.

"Better I find the problem," Fareedh answered.

"Did you account for *Majera's* mass?" Peter said suddenly.

"Oh crap."

Shari sounded annoyed, "Yeah, 'Oh crap' is what I like to hear."

"Sorry," Fareedh said. "I thought something was off. Give me a sec. I'll make a quick patch."

It took just a few minutes. Then he stretched and said, "You can toggle between the two configurations now: with and without *Majera* on board."

"Got it."

The thrusters went on again, and this time there were no objections, exclamations, or alarms. Instead, the big ship slowed a little bit, sliding into a higher orbit. The whole maneuver took a matter of minutes.

"I think this is going to work," Shari commed. I watched her work her console a moment. "New calculations show we've got twenty three minutes to retro if we want to go down easy," she added.

Unger's gentle voice came from right behind me, causing me to jump, "We should get the others onboard."

"Everyone hear that?" I called.

There was a chorus of acknowledgements, and the lights in the display representing people on the *Émilie* began converging on the axis shaft. In less than two minutes, the airlock started cycling. Inside of ten, a rattle of conversation was growing behind me in the wardroom. I got up to count heads.

Peter squeezed past me at the wardroom door to take his seat on the bridge. I wrinkled my nose as he did; he'd been in his suit for a long time, and it had been longer since he'd seen the inside of his Cleaner. Well, I probably didn't smell like snowdrops either. After Peter cleared my view, I saw *Majera* was going to be a crowded ship for a while. There were nine people crammed into our common room: Sirena, Marta, and seven others I didn't recognize. None of them were children, which struck me as odd. I'd have thought they would have taken priority. I also noted that neither the engineer twins nor the doctor were here.

"Where are the rest?" I called to Unger, still on the bridge.

The minister turned to face me. "Marie and Jean are staying aboard to help Shari in case trouble arises. Lucas as well."

I nodded. "Alright, welcome aboard, everyone. I'm afraid we don't have chairs for all of you, but it's not likely to be a bumpy ride. With any luck, we'll be down on the surface in an hour." I pointed to the kitchen area in the corner, partially obscured by a pair of *Glorieux*: a tall, sturdy-looking woman and a delicate young man. "Help yourself to the Maker. We've got plenty of goop."

Unger brushed past me from behind into the wardroom, gave me a grateful smile, and said, "I'll see to their needs."

Marta and Sirena made their way to where I was, the princess ducking her head and simply flying over the big table in the middle.

"I hope you don't mind if I ride in front, darling," Sirena said. "I've gotten used to it."

"You pay the bills," I said, answering her smile.

Marta gave me a sweaty hug on the way to her seat, and I was vaguely aware that I didn't mind her scent the way I minded Peter's. I gave Unger a sloppy salute before taking my position on the bridge.

"Five minutes," Shari commed. "You'd better get going."

I chewed my lip. We were ready. No problems with the pre-flight check. The Tree winked bright green at me. All systems were Go. Still I hesitated. I knew Shari was right, that she was the right person for the job, and that I had to bring up the rear... but still, leaving the *Émilie* felt like running out on them.

I felt a gentle touch on my wrist. Pinky had encircled it with one of his 'hands'. "It's okay," he said softly. "We've done what we can. Let's see them home."

My eyes stung a moment, and I put my free hand over his. I nodded and cleared my throat.

"This is *Majera*," I said. "I'm opening the hangar door. Godspeed, *Émilie*."

The big portal irised open above us, and the thin trace of air on the deck we'd vented earlier puffed away into space. Pinky had already unfastened the physical ties, all that was left was to disengage the magnetic anchors and retract the nose skid. I did so, tapped the thrusters, and in moments, we were out in open space.

I kept *Majera* close, no more than a few hundred meters. It was enough distance in case something weird happened, but close enough that I had a good view of the *Émilie*.

Then came the tricky part.

The *Émilie* was whizzing over the planet at more than 7,000 meters per second. The colony ship had to bleed all that speed off before trying to land, but at the same time, not go into the atmosphere. The *Émilie* didn't have an aerodynamic shape or any kind of heat shield. If it plunged downward, it'd burn up like a meteor.

Shari began using the antigravity to decelerate almost as soon as *Majera* had gotten clear, the giant ship thrusting just over one gee against its current path. With the antigravity out on most of the *Émilie*, they couldn't risk more than that for fear of putting too much strain on the ship.

Émilie slowed down at a rate of 12 meters per second. To keep from sinking, the huge cylinder began to tilt its back end toward the planet, resisting the force of the planet's gravity as it bled the speed that kept it aloft. I did the same with *Majera*, keeping our position relative to the *Émilie* steady. It was a lot easier for me than Shari—we could handle two gees with ease for short stretches, and more.

The minutes ticked by. At the start of the braking, the *Émilie* had been a dark blot against the skies, illuminated only by running lights, but by the time she had turned to be diagonal to the planet's surface, the sun had crested the edge of the planet, bathing the behemoth in a dazzle of light. That was part of the plan; we didn't want to try to land in the dark. It did mean cutting our safety margin to about twenty minutes, though. If we didn't land safely by then, it meant people would start waking up in mid-flight—before we had a chance to let the air in.

Peter peered at his console, watching the *Émilie's* heartbeat for any signs of trouble. I saw the sheen of sweat on his wide forehead, and a muscle twitched in his temple. Shari commed us every thirty seconds. All was well. So far. Her voice, and my reply, were the only words spoken as we flew together into daylight.

After fifteen minutes, the *Émilie* was now standing almost on its end, its orbital velocity bled. The only thing holding up our two ships was about a gee of antigravity thrust pointing straight down. Below us, the vast continent we'd briefly explored loomed brown and faded green. A wave of clouds had come in since we'd been down there.

"Low pressure system," Marta said, looking over my shoulder. "It'll be raining in a few days."

I grunted in reply. Whatever happened would be long over by then.

"I'm ready to begin the descent," Shari commed. If she was scared, there was no trace of it in her voice.

"I'll be right beside you," I answered.

Émilie began falling below us. Shari had cut her antigravity thrust to almost nothing, letting the planet accelerate the ship without resistance. I did the same, and our speed quickly built up. 10 seconds went by. 20 seconds. I started to get nervous. We were coming up on 1,000 kilometers an hour.

"When are you going to bring your power back?" I asked, a catch in my throat.

"I want to get through as quick as we can," came the reply. "I'm restoring thrust now."

The *Émilie*'s antigravity repelled the planet below with a force equal to the gravity pulling down on the ship. Now the ship would sink at a constant speed, the two forces balanced. *Majera* sailed past under the *Émilie* until I compensated with higher thrust.

I got us level with the *Émilie* in short order. It was all very smooth compared to the last time I'd zoomed through this atmosphere. There was no shuddering, no fireballs. Through the Window, the giant ship wasn't even glowing or anything, just outlined crisply against the still-black sky. Outside, the temperature was nearly 1,000° K, but the air up here was so thin that it was still practically a vacuum. It wouldn't last, though. At this speed, we'd be on the ground in less than half an hour.

Reflexively, I took a look at the fuel gauge. Using the antigravity for thrust was less efficient than the engines, enough so that we never used antigravity to get from planet to planet; that's what our big engine was for. But for take-offs and landings, antigravity was a lot more comfortable—and in this case, we didn't have a choice. The *Émilie* didn't have a reaction engine at all, so we had to use antigrav to keep station with them. It didn't matter though; we had plenty of fuel, and even if we were low after landing, there was an ocean to draw from. As for the *Émilie*'s fuel situation, Decks 6 through 8 were devoted to nothing but compressed hydrogen, and there had been enough in their tanks for a trip home if the planet hadn't panned out. They had enough to get them to the ground, for certain.

Majera and *Émilie* continued downward, only the dropping altitude numbers and the slow growing of the ground betraying our descent. Near the 150 kilometer mark, I caught a flicker of motion. As I watched, a bright glow began to encase the bigger ship, gentle and blue. It wavered from the bottom to the top in broad waves, little curls flashing off the sides. Flames.

I panicked. "Is everything all right over there?" I blurted.

"What do you mean? Everything's fine," Shari said.

"You look like you're on *fire*."

There was an ominous silence. Then Jean's voice cut in. "We're not on fire, *you* are." This made my stomach sink about half a meter until I heard the laugh the engineer followed up his comment with. "Relax, Kitra. It's just ionization. Between the thruster and all the charged particles, we're making a local aurora. It's quite beautiful, actually."

I looked over at Peter. He turned at the sound of my chair's swiveling. "You might have told me this was to be expected," I said.

He spread his hands in a shrug. "I didn't know."

Even as I turned back to look at the *Émilie*, the glow was starting to fade, going away just as I could appreciate how pretty it was.

The outside temperature dropped fast as we approached 100 kilometers. At the same time, the air pressure finally reached a full pascal. The sky was still black, but we were now definitely in the atmosphere. A loud *spang* hit my ears, and I instinctively gripped at the flight sticks before realizing the sound hadn't come from the *Majera*, but over the comms. The sharp report was followed by an ominous creaking.

"It's the hull," Marie commed before I could ask. "The pressure and the cold, I think."

I looked over at Pinky and whispered, "I don't remember this happening when it got dark in orbit."

He gave me a three-armed shrug in reply. "If weird noises bugged you, you'd have tossed me overboard a long time ago."

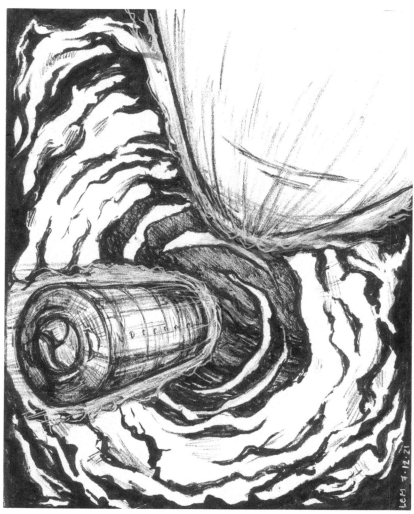

*"You look like you're on **fire**."*

"Not on your life," I said with a little smile. "You're staying, raspberries and all."

Another sound, like the sound of beam artillery arcing through the air, made me jump.

"Hull remains uncompromised," Jean said.

I felt a broad hand on my shoulder. Peter's. "If they're still talking, they're fine. *Émilie's* a tough ship." In a lower voice, he added, "Anyway, if they go, it'll be all at once and nothing first."

"Big comfort, Peter."

"Sorry."

I kept my eyes glued to *Émilie*, as if I could keep that ship together by will alone. It seemed to work as well as anything else; for now, the big cylinder remained intact. The deep gray skin of the ship started to sparkle as frost condensed on it. The horizon flattened and the sky turned indigo. The control sticks started to buck in my hands. It was that jet stream we'd encountered on the way down last time, threatening to tumble us. I turned *Majera* into the wind and pushed the thrusters, just a touch, to stabilize the ship.

Just in time to see the great bulk of the colony ship looming in the Window. It was coming straight at us, blown by the powerful breeze like a balloon in the wind. I heard a squeak from behind me as I increased downward thrust, trying to get us over the *Émilie*. The other ship blew by underneath, missing by too few meters for comfort. By the time I had them centered in the Window again, they were cruising sideways across the landscape at more than 50 meters per second.

"You're drifting with the stream," Fareedh called.

Shari's voice was taut, "I know. I can't do anything about it. I'm afraid to angle us against it."

"Is this going to be okay?" I asked Pinky.

"As long as they keep going down, it doesn't matter much where we land. It's all pretty flat." He paused, consulting his maps. "Well, until they hit the ocean."

"Great," I said. "What's the margin for error?"

"10 minutes?"

I called up the atmosphere map from our first trip. We *might* be below the high winds of the stratosphere in 10 minutes. Then again, we might not.

"Shari, you might want to go through this layer a little faster to reduce the drift," I called.

She answered, "If I cut braking thrust to speed up, we'll have to go at higher thrust at the end to shed the extra velocity."

"Do you know how to swim?"

Silence. Then, "I take your point." A moment later, the *Émilie* began to shrink as it sped faster below us. I cut our braking thrust to match their descent rate.

This was actually fine, I told myself as I wrestled with the control sticks to keep us aligned with the refugee ship. Anything that increased the time we had to wake everyone up safely was a good thing. So long as Shari didn't crash in the process.

Marta must have been thinking along the same lines. "Jean," she called, "where are we in the revival process?"

The doctor's voice came through jittery. He was up beyond the controlled gravity section and must have been enduring a bumpy ride. "The pre-conditioning checks have been completed on all decks. The bed systems are primed to inject the metabolism speeders. When that happens, we'll want to get the doctors back on here as quickly as possible."

"The doctors?" I asked. Ah. That's why there weren't any children among those we'd taken on board. All of the revived would be *Glorieux* who could help with the other refugees. "Oh, right. I got it."

Below us, the edge of the coastline grew closer and closer. Before it passed directly beneath us, the incessant tugging I'd been fighting abruptly stopped. Almost immediately, I heard a grunt over the comms as the *Émilie* poured on the thrust to decelerate. We zipped past the ship, and I slowly drifted up parallel to it again. We were only 7,500 meters above the ground now, and the sky was a brilliant blue. The chorus of creaks and groaning metal was a constant background over our communications. Shari called out the altitude every hundred meters now.

I wiped the sweat off my forehead as I checked on our braking thrust. Already up to 1.3g, and we were still falling too fast. We'd need to thrust more if we were going to land safely. *Majera* could handle it, but could the *Émilie*? I had nightmare visions of the unchecked Deck 2 splitting open, breaking the refugee ship in two.

3,000 meters. 2,000 meters. The ground below us stopped being a map of itself and turned into a landscape. We were close enough to the ocean that I could see the breakers as parallel lines of silver. Pinky had picked the area well. The coastal plain was pretty smooth from here on inward for dozens of kilometers. There was no way to know if the swath of green below was solid ground or a swamp, though. For a moment, I thought of zooming below the *Émilie's* projected landing path and testing the dirt. But for one thing, there wasn't enough time, and for another, it didn't make much difference. It wasn't like the giant ship could fly anywhere else.

There was a huge clang over the comms as we hit 500 meters. "What was that," Peter exclaimed.

"I don't know," answered Jean worriedly. "Probably a loose piece of machinery. We're at 1.5g."

The ground rushed up at us. I wanted to reach out and brake the *Émilie* myself somehow, that feeling one gets as a passenger in a manually piloted car, and just as useless. At 100 meters, the thrum of the *Émilie's* thrusters edged out of the subsonic range and became audible over the comms, setting my teeth on edge. But at last, we had slowed down to a tolerable speed. I took another look. The ground seemed flat enough, no big hills to knock the big ship cockeyed.

"Twenty meters," Shari called. "Fifteen. Ten. Eight. Five. Four. Holding. Kitra, how are we looking?" For the first time, tension cracked her voice.

I brought *Majera* down to just above the ground cover, close enough to see individual stalks. "There are a couple of big bushes underneath you."

Marta piped in, "That's probably a good thing. It may mean more solid ground."

A heavy sigh over the comms. Then, "Here goes nothing."

The huge vessel closed the gap between itself and the ground with maddening slowness. At last, they made touchdown. I let out a huge breath and started to smile.

There was another groan of metal as the *Émilie* descended another several meters and started to tilt sideways.

"You're not stable," Fareedh called loudly.

A gout of water splashed out from the edge of the refugee ship. They *were* in a swamp, or the water table was very close to the surface.

"I know," Shari shouted. "I can't find the bottom."

Pinky flipped on the deep radar and peered at orange-outlined landscape. "There is no bottom. You're essentially on a sandbar."

Shari uttered something short and indecipherable. Probably a phrase unique to Gloire.

Peter said, "You can either let it go and hope it holds you, or..."

"Or I can keep the engines on at one gee. Hold on."

The thruster thrum, which had faded, came back to life and the colony ship ponderously straightened out again.

"Look," Shari said. "I think I can keep her like this. The plant and thruster are still reading green. Let's get the people and equipment safely out, and then I can let her go. If we're lucky, we'll just settle into the mud straight. If we're not..."

Unger had come up behind me and was gripping my seat. "Can't you move inland? If the ship is lost, we'll lose much of the colony's power."

"Boss," Shari commed, "If I try maneuvering the ship down here, it's just as likely I'll tip it over. It wasn't built for this."

The minister sighed. "Very well. How much time left until the revival process begins?"

Lucas answered quickly, "It's beginning. We've got to get air in here in the next five minutes."

I felt the fingers of my right hand start rubbing together. It was a good thing we'd raced through the jet stream. There hadn't been any margin for error after all.

"I'm opening up the hangar door," Marie called. "There." Her voice was filled with relief.

There were exhales all around, and Fareedh thumped me on the shoulder so I'd turn and see his grin. We'd done it! Now we just needed to get the doctors on board to help with the reviving. I engaged the thrusters and zoomed our little ship up alongside the great bulk of the *Émilie*, cresting the upper edge of the refugee ship in moments.

The hangar door wasn't open.

Lucas commed before I had a chance to say anything. "We're not getting any air in the ship. What's going on?"

"The ship's *sayar* says the bay is open!" I heard Marie exclaim.

"It's not," I said. "It's shut tight."

"I'm recycling the system," the engineer commed. Then, with a curse, she said, "It's not working. Now it's not showing me anything."

"Maybe it's the pressure differential," Peter started to ramble, "or the ship's *sayar* code is broken."

"It doesn't matter," Unger said, voice hoarse. "We've got to get air to them."

"Sixty seconds to first lock disengage," Lucas said, his voice tight. "That'll vent the air the sleepers have in their beds, leaving them in vacuum."

"Fareedh?" I cried out.

He was tapping uselessly at his console. "I'm locked out of the system from here."

My mind raced. We had to get that door open. If it wasn't going to open by itself, we'd have to force the thing. A welder? No, that'd take too long. Explosives? We didn't have any. Ram the hatch with *Majera*? Sure, and risk losing the only way back to civilization.

What else? My eyes darted along the console. The cheery lights of the Tree, all but one glowing green, caught my eye, held it. All but one of the lights... I thumped my arm rest. Of course! Our innocent, completely utilitarian comm laser, the one we'd gotten to deal with pirates. It could push megawatts of beamed power into a friendly ship as easily as an enemy.

"Hang on," I called. "I'm going to blow the hatch." I called up the comm laser's targeting system and locked the crosshairs on the center of the hatch.

"Good thinking, darling," I heard behind me.

"It was your idea," I pointed out. I activated the laser, and a beam of green light speared out from our ship, hitting the *Émilie*'s hatch. Nothing. It might as well have been a flashlight for all the effect it was having. I boosted the power to maximum and shifted the frequency higher, into the one legal ultraviolet band. The beam faded from view. Anxious seconds went by. A scorch mark appeared, quickly expanded. Glitter appeared around it. Pieces of vaporized metal, or maybe ionized air. I kept my finger on the trigger, ready to switch off quickly. It wouldn't do to burn through anything vital.

All at once, the entire hatch blew inward. A split second later, I heard a loud "oof" from Lucas' comm. I switched off the laser.

"Have you got air?" Marta cried.

"Nearly knocked me off my feet," was the doctor's breathless reply. "Yes, full pressure."

That was followed by a muffled crash. "I think that was the hatch," Shari commed. "But we're fine," she added. "Holding steady, and we've got air here, too."

"Yes!" came a bellow from my right. I turned, and Pinky had extended all three arms up, their ends balled into huge fists. I couldn't help but grin.

"Let's get you some help, Lucas!" I called out, and I slid *Majera* to hover over the hole where the hatch had been.

"How are we going to get people down there?" said Fareedh doubtfully, "We can't land the ship on the *Émilie*."

He was right. With the *Émilie* keeping upright only through positive thrust, it would be dangerous to lock ourselves to it. But that meant there was no easy way to get inside. Plus, if the lift system in the axis shaft *had* been working before, the hatch had probably knocked it out. The *Émilie* was a skyscraper twenty stories tall with no easy way to get between levels.

"Leave it to me, darling," Sirena said. I set *Majera's* autopilot to keep us fixed above the *Émilie* and turned around.

"What are you going to do?" I asked.

"Simple," she said, raising a dainty hand with a shrug. "I can fly. I'll bring them down one at a time, each to a different deck. Undignified, perhaps, but it will get the job done."

"You're a miracle," Marta said, giving the princess a quick hug.

"So true, so true. Off I go." And with that, she glided into the wardroom.

"There are heavy duty antigrav carts on Deck 3," Unger said. "Jean and Marie can activate them for offloading passengers and equipment."

The light flashed indicating the airlock cycling, and there was a little cheer as we watched Sirena flit off from the *Majera* and into the *Émilie*. It was unreal. We'd done it. We'd saved everyone. So long as Shari could keep the refugee ship upright, the rest was logistics.

A tingle went up my spine accompanied by yet another lurch in the pit of my stomach. And if she couldn't, the ship would tumble and everyone on board would be lost. I shook my head. No, I didn't believe that would happen, not with all we'd been through.

But I mouthed a little prayer. Just to be sure.

Unloading the refugees took the better part of a day. The sun was now on the opposite end of the sky, and the *Émilie's* lengthening shadow extended far along the coastline. A milling crowd of *Glorieux* covered the more-or-less solid ground inland of the giant ship. Some were already inside a huge inflatable shelter, unloaded along with the first wave of awakened refugees and erected in less than ten minutes. Others were using portable blasters and a couple of dirtmovers to carve a waste disposal system out of the bare earth.

For hours, a never ending stream of people and equipment had gone from the top of the cylindrical vessel to the ground, carried on the four transport disks that still worked out of the five on board. About a fifth of all the rest of *Émilie's* equipment was also inoperative; the machines that didn't work were left onboard.

I shaded my eyes to watch the crews arranging the unloaded machines into some sort of order. The wind was picking up, whipping the waves into whitecaps. It felt — and smelled — good after weeks of recycled air. Even Marta's best efforts hadn't quite kept *Majera* from getting a little ripe. I looked back at the *Émilie* in time to watch the next load emerge from the rim of the ship. For the last couple of hours, it had been equipment, all of the people long since unloaded.

The roar of the colony ship's power plant had gotten louder throughout the day. It was almost unbearable now. It was clear that the current situation couldn't last much longer.

"They can't have a lot left," Fareedh said, his voice raised over the din. He'd stayed with me near the parked *Majera* along with Pinky; Peter, Marta, and Sirena were at the growing camp lending a hand.

"Last I heard, some of the stuff on Deck 4 was still jammed in," I replied, rubbing my hands against my shorts. "I wish we could help."

"They have plenty of people," Pinky observed. The dark swirls of his eyespots widened in his otherwise blank 'face.' "Did you see that?"

"That's the second time," Fareedh said.

"What?" I asked.

"The *Émilie*. She wobbled," Pinky said.

I called into my *sayar*, "Shari, Pinky says you're unstable."

It took a moment for the engineer to reply. She wasn't in her makeshift control cabin anymore, having left the system on automatic after stabilizing the ship. Patching into her display, I could see the holo trembling. "Yeah, believe me, we know," she said at last.

Unger's voice came through the comms, "You've got to get out of there."

Shari grunted. "Half the medical equipment is left."

"You have twenty people in there. They're more important." The minister's voice brooked no disagreement.

"Copy that. Gathering the chicks now." This was followed by a grunt as the *Émilie* shuddered, a pulse that started from the base and ran to the top. A gabble of cries filled the comms as the unloading crew ran for the hover disk parked in the axis shaft. The rumble of the thruster became a rising whine so piercing I had to cover my ears. Pinky, who didn't have that luxury, trembled amber-shaded for a moment, then dashed back into the *Majera*.

An almost living cry came from the trembling refugee ship, now visibly listing. All at once, the shriek of the thruster was gone and the *Émilie* was falling. The giant ship settled into the mud with a delayed *whump*. At first, it seemed that the ground would hold the vessel upright, but slowly, inexorably, the ship began to tilt seaward with a horrible mechanical groan that drowned out everything else. A puff of smoke exploded out the top, obscuring the upper section from view.

"Shari!" I shouted. "Are you clear?"

There was no response.

I watched in horror as the *Émilie* arced toward the ocean, then closed my eyes. I couldn't bear to look. Moments later, I heard the agony of sheared metal as the ship crashed along the beach and waves. My knees gave out, and I fell sobbing to the ground. Shari... Jean and Marie... *Lord, no...*

I felt a thump on my shoulder, someone clapping their hands against it. I opened my eyes to see Fareedh grinning like a madman. I wanted to scream. Had he gone insane? Twenty people had just died!

He pointed upward, shouting something I couldn't hear through the ringing in my ears.

A round shadow, barely visible against the purpling sky, twinkled with the last rays of the sun. A transport disk. Shari's disk!

Fareedh hunched down next to me, gripping my shoulders. He was still yelling soundlessly, but the meaning was clear. They'd made it.

We'd made it.

Chapter 16

The warm rays of the sun beat down on the new sheltered cove that lay in the lee of the tumbled *Émilie*. I tread water lazily, the salt of the ocean keeping me afloat without much work. The waters in the sea off Denizli are cold, fed by an arctic stream. Here, it was just a shade cooler than bathwater. I thrilled at the openness, the *outside* of it all. The front of clouds we'd spotted on our way down was a dark line on the horizon, threatening a storm tomorrow. But not today.

It was about as close to heaven as I could imagine. For the first time in forever, it was just me and my friends, like we used to be. Well, not quite: we had a new friend in the mix. Sirena bobbed near me, her arms perfectly still, red hair glistening with water. She was the only one of us not wearing a swimsuit, but she wore nudity like a royal gown. As I watched, she leaped into the air, describing a perfect arc, and splashed into the water, head first, followed by torso, hips, and a long bronze tail.

I watched admiringly. I had known about the people of Atlántida and their particular solution to living on an ocean planet; Sirena had told me why she had to use a grav chair right at the start. But she'd always swam in private, and I certainly wasn't going to be nosy. It was a beautiful thing, seeing the princess in her natural environment, and she glowed with joy.

Speaking of beautiful things...

Marta had made for herself a suit out of something blue and shiny. It didn't cover much, and there was a lot of her, and despite resolutions and common sense, I found myself staring. Blushing, I sank neck deep in the water. She seemed not to notice, her attention currently divided between Fareedh and Peter, who were treading water side by side. They contrasted even more with their shirts off: Fareedh was dark and wiry, while Peter was twice as wide and so pale he looked like he glowed in the dark.

A stream of water got me right in the ear. I squealed and turned away, the spray continuing on the back of my neck. It was like a hose. It stopped, and when I'd gotten myself turned around, Pinky was tinted bright salmon with amusement.

"You... you beachball!" I shouted, splashing him back.

"What happened?" Marta asked.

"Pinky squirted me. I don't even want to know from where."

The alien zipped out of my range with ease, trailing a foam of bubbles. From a safe distance, he called out, "I'll have you know that was a gift from the bottom of my heart."

Both Peter and Fareedh chorused "eww," while Marta, made of stronger stuff, giggled.

Pinky raised two pseudopods and linked them in a victory sign like an ancient gladiator just as Sirena absolutely *doused* him with a flick of her flukes. It was like a targeted rainstorm. She surfaced, and I called out, "My hero!" She curled a thin arm over her chest and bowed.

"I see war has been declared," Pinky intoned ominously, "and we're now in an arms race." His appendages grew curled flippers and dipped into the water.

Peter pointed up at the sky. "Heads up. We have company."

"I won't fall for so clear a ruse," Pinky said, winding up.

"No, he's right," Marta said. "Look."

I followed their gaze and saw a quickly growing circle in the sky. One of the transport disks was sailing toward us. Squinting, I made out Unger at the front, and it looked like Shari in the driver seat. They waved as the disk came to a halt nearby, a meter or so above the calm water.

Peter called out to Shari, "How's the bump?"

The engineer rubbed at the clear bandage that swathed the upper right part of her head. She'd gotten the wound dodging the debris on her mad disc ride out of the *Émilie*. It was amazing no one else had gotten injured. She was a hero.

"Hurts, but it's no big deal. It's in a lot better shape than that thing." She waved her hand over at the crushed hulk that had once been an interstellar refugee ship, a broken pile of junk that sank under the waves about two thirds along its length. "Did you find out what happened to your crack in the universe?"

Peter shrugged his broad shoulders, sinking momentarily into the water. "I don't think it's there anymore. I'd have to dig through a few hundred tons of stuff to be sure, but..."

Marta swam over to squeeze his arm. "Sorry about your thesis."

He grinned shyly down at her. "I got data, no problem. Honestly, I'd rather it *not* be around."

"You came a long way," I said to the pair on the disk. "What's up?"

"You didn't answer your *sayar*," Unger said with an amused smile. The minister looked better, the gray of worry gone from the wrinkled face. "You look like you're having fun."

"Your timing was perfect," Fareedh said, gently treading water. "You stopped the first inter-species conflict on the planet."

"What conflict? All-around peace-lovers here!" came Pinky's reply. He'd reverted to an almost perfectly spherical shape and was bobbing innocently on the swell.

"Actually, with regard to the planet..." Unger began, low voice now more serious, "it occurs to me that it could use a name. After all, we've been able to complete our mission to make this our new home."

That sounded ominous. Now that they were safe, were they going to become like the Puritans and chase us off?

"I thought you'd registered it as 'New Gloire'," Fareedh said. I noticed Pinky turn a pale shade of disapproving yellow. At least he was tactful enough not to raspberry.

Unger nodded. "That had been the original plan, yes, but given the circumstances, we felt a new name was appropriate." The minister's eyes flickered to Sirena. "No, deserving. You had come here, like us, hoping to find a new home for your people. You could have abandoned us to our fate, but instead you sacrificed your goal to aid us in ours. It is no hyperbole that you," Unger's gaze swept to include all of us before returning to the princess, "all of you, have earned our undying gratitude and friendship."

"It was nothing less than our obligation to morality," Sirena said with a smooth formality that bordered on ritual.

"Nevertheless," Unger pressed on, "no good deed should go un-rewarded. I've had my experts draw up an amendment to our charter. More of a complete revision, really. You can read it at your leisure of course, but the main thrust is that we would like to open the planet to the people of Atlántida. It's a huge world. There is certainly no reason we cannot co-reside in prosperity, particularly given your, shall we say, aquatic bent."

My face cracked into a smile. The *Glorieux* would have been well within their rights to thank us for our help and then keep the planet to themselves. The second they'd made planetfall, the world was legally theirs. Now they were offering to share it.

Unger wasn't done, though. "Beyond that, I think it only just that this planet's name reflect the person whose expedition made the con-tinuation of Gloire at all possible, and whose appellation happens to be singularly appropriate for this water-blessed world." The Minis-ter's face creased into a grin that made all the wrinkles turn into laugh lines. "We would like to call the world 'Sirena,' if that be acceptable."

All eyes were on the princess. If it'd been me, I'd have whooped with joy. But she simply bowed her head slightly and said, in the same clear tones she'd used before, "On behalf of Atlántida, I accept your proposal. I also accept the renaming of the world."

I looked back at Unger, who seemed a little disappointed at the muted reaction, not quite sure what to say next.

But Sirena wasn't done. Her stiff proclamation was followed, af-ter a deliberate pause, by a wink. "You have excellent taste, darling," she said with a smile.

Shari barked out a laugh that turned into a suppressed snort as Unger looked woundedly at her. But the smile quickly returned to the minister's face.

"I would ask one final favor," Unger said. "I imagine you will be returning to your people to convey the news of our agreement. If it is not too much trouble, we'd be grateful if you could inform our agent on Hyvilma as to the current state of our mission and apprise her of our amended contract."

Sirena turned to me. "What do you think? Perhaps you could of-fer Their Excellency a discount on your courier fee since you'll be headed that way anyway."

I grinned. "Oh... I *suppose*. Hey Pinky. What *is* our courier fee, anyway?"

"Ten vials of subliming ester," he answered promptly.

Peter splashed him. "That's *your* fee. Kitra gets paid in coffee."

"I... I'm afraid we don't have much to spare," Unger said seriously.

I waved a careless, dripping hand. "Given the circumstances, I think I can waive my personal fee." An idea occurred to me then. "How about *Majera* gets free refueling rights on Sirena? The planet, I mean. You've got lots of water to spare."

Shari nudged Unger in the ribs. "We can do that, eh boss?"

The minister nodded. "That we can do."

"It's a deal!" I called out.

Unger smoothed out their long dress tunic. "Well, that's settled then. We'll leave you to your fun. When you get back to shore, we've got a small ceremony planned. I hope you don't mind a little celebrity."

Pinky extended a pseudopod to wave. "Oh, we'll manage, somehow."

Shari levitated the disk a few meters before calling out, "I'm getting a swimsuit. Don't come back before I can join you!"

After Shari and Unger had dwindled to a point, I turned to the crew. "You know what this means, right?"

"We'll learn Shari's taste in swimwear?" Fareedh ventured.

Marta tapped him lightly on the shoulder. "It means we've pushed the Frontier out a few parsecs all by ourselves." She looked over at me. "Right?"

"It sure does," I said. "With this planet as a base, there are dozens more worlds to explore."

Marta chimed in eagerly, "Exotic biomes."

"Beautiful starscapes," Fareedh added.

"Endless gaming opportunities," said Pinky.

"Yet more chances for equipment to fail," noted Peter.

Sirena arced backward and fluttered her tail on the water, creating a momentary rainbow of spray. "It all sounds delightful, I must say. I shall be sad to part company after we return to Hyvilma."

My smile faded as her words sank in. "That's right. You're…" I swallowed, "you're not staying on with us." There was no keeping the disappointment out of my voice. I'd gotten so used to the princess as one of the crew, and as a friend. I had trouble picturing us as a five-person crew again. It was inevitable, deep down I knew that, but knowing and acceptance were two different things.

She glided gracefully over to me, reaching out a dainty hand. I took it.

"All good things end. And in this case, the ending comes with a fresh beginning." Her lips quirked into a soft smile as she looked over at Marta. "And you, for one, certainly must be happy at the prospect of getting Peter's gadgets out of your room."

"There is that," she giggled. "Still, it's been a lot of fun. I've learned a lot from you, Dr. de la Atlántida."

Peter snickered, "Some internship."

"Not just the medical insights," Marta went on. "She's a terrific action-adventure hero."

"I did rather exert myself, didn't I?"

"We're going to miss you, Your Highness," Fareedh said. "It truly was an honor and a privilege."

She waved her hand dismissively. "Now, now, darling. You're starting to sound like Their Grace. So stuffy." Turning back to me, she frowned slightly at what she saw. She pulled in close, wrapping me in a warm hug. Then she clasped my shoulders and kissed both of my cheeks. "I will never forget what you, all of you, have done for us. Thank you, from the bottom of my heart. This world will always be open to you, and I'm sure you will be regular visitors. Moreover, we shall always be friends." The smile returned, "After all, you are my second Consuelo."

I blushed and looked down, speechless. I may have had tears in my eyes. It was hard to tell with the salt spray and all.

"In any event, we still have two weeks together," she continued, turning to face the others. "After all, you do need to take me at least as far as Hyvilma. We'll make the most of it. Indeed, I might even be persuaded to play that ridiculously long game you like to play. *Empires*, was it?"

I couldn't help grinning at that. "Oh, you're on," I said.

"Speaking of games," Pinky boomed, "this is all very touching, but the parsnips remain unbuttered. I came here to play, and I still intend to." He grew another arm and placed huge palms over his eye-spots. "Now then... Marco!"

"Polo!" Fareedh and Peter chorused.

Sirena gave my shoulder a final squeeze, then sang out, "Challenge accepted. Polo!" She dove under the surface without a splash, and I kicked my feet to put some distance between me and Pinky. The princess surfaced silently next to Marta, who gave her a brief hug. Sirena was right. The next two weeks would be a lot of fun, and the years after that. This wasn't goodbye, just a brief parting of the ways. We'd be back, to see her, and to push the boundaries of the known universe even further out. Maybe she'd even join us on another trip someday.

I couldn't wait.

About the Series

Back when my father was a kid, they had science fiction books for young adults and kids. They called them "juveniles," and they usually featured a young hero flying to the stars. I grew up on these and loved them.

Over the years, YA became all about dystopia and fantasy. I enjoyed The Hunger Games and Harry Potter as much as everyone else, but I missed the space adventures. I wanted to see stories that weren't zero-sum game fights against a Big Bad, that featured reasonably accurate science and characters who struggled with realistic problems. Tales of friendship, ingenuity, and wonder.

Kitra was my first book. It was more successful than I could have dreamed. A year and a half after it came out, it was *still* getting glowing reviews. It resonated with people. The found family, the diversity in representation, the "strange new worlds", Pinky's jokes, all of these made readers happy again and again.

But there was one common refrain: people wanted to know more. About *Kitra* and her ragtag crew. The nature of Pinky. The planets beyond the Frontier.

And so, *Sirena*. I hope you enjoy it as much as I enjoyed creating it!

~

The lifeblood of every author is audience feedback. Please consider leaving a review (of whatever length) on Amazon, GoodReads, or your favorite platform.

About the Publisher

Founded in 2019 by Galactic Journey's Gideon Marcus, Journey Press publishes the best science fiction, current and classic, with an emphasis on the unusual and the diverse. We also partner with other small presses to offer exciting titles we know you'll like!

Also available from Journey Press:

Kitra by Gideon Marcus
A YA Space Adventure

Stranded in space: no fuel, no way home—and no one coming to help!

Nineteen-year-old Kitra Yilmaz dreams of traveling the galaxy like her Ambassador mother. But soaring in her glider is the closest she can get to touching the stars, until she stakes her inheritance on a salvage Navy spaceship—and ends up light years away from anywhere.

I Want the Stars by Tom Purdom
A Timeless Classic

Fleeing a utopian Earth, searching for meaning, Jenorden and his friends take to the stars to save a helpless race from merciless telepathic aliens.

Hugo Finalist Tom Purdom's 1964 epic is a progressive masterpiece in the vein of Samuel R. Delany's Babel-17.

Sibyl Sue Blue by Rosel George Brown
The Original Woman Space Detective

Who she is: Sibyl Sue Blue, single mom, undercover detective, and damn good at her job.

What she wants: to solve the mysterious benzale murders, prevent more teenage deaths, and maybe find her long-lost husband.

How she'll get it: seduce a millionaire, catch a ride on his spaceship, and crack the case at the edge of the known galaxy.

CPSIA information can be obtained
at www.ICGtesting.com
Printed in the USA
LVHW090234050222
710188LV00001B/60